"Brendan Detzner's vibrant
looking for the perfect colle

-Wayne Allen Sallee

"Brendan Detzner's best stories start with some of the most familiar tropes of horror and science fiction. Haunted trees, mysterious stage magicians, sentient computers, and talking skeletons are all in evidence, as well as sea monsters, invisible friends, and a twisted variation on the old Jekyll & Hyde story. But then he surprises the reader, again and again, by refusing to take us down the familiar paths, instead opting for side roads that most of us never even noticed were there. Contained in this collection are sixteen tales of the truly unexpected. Highly recommended for fans of experimental horror."

-Michael Penkas

"Detzner will creep yer shit out. Have spare drawers when you read him."

-Patty Templeton, author of *There Is No Lovely End*

EJ-
From one secret master of Forest Park to another.

Best,

Brendan

BEASTS

16 MORE WEIRD STORIES BY BRENDAN DETZNER

"In The Fall" originally appeared in One Buck Horror Volume 5, June 2012

"The Sasquatch Vs. Chupacabra Variations" originally appeared in Bizarrocast Episode 37, December 2013

"A Day and Two Night When I Was Twenty" originally appeared in Untied Shoelaces of the Mind Issue 7, December 2012

"Two Nights Only" originally appeared in Tales to Terrify No. 95, November 2013

"Wetwork" originally appeared in Kaleidotrope, Winter 2013

"The Gardener Estate" originally appeared in Body Parts, May 2015

"The Specimen" originally appeared in The Dream Quarry Volume 2, June 2014

"Shadow" originally appeared in Edge of Propinquity, March 2009

"Beasts" by Brendan Detzner is licensed under a Creative Commons Attribution-NonCommercial-Sharealike 3.0 Unported License
ISBN 978-1-329-13016-6

Table of Contents

5- In the Fall

12- The Chupacabra Versus Sasquatch Variations 1-9

18- Spirits of the Wind

48- A Day and Two Nights When I Was Twenty

54- The Return of Uncle Hungry's Pizza Time Fun Band

58- I-65

66- Two Nights Only

73- PCBF

81- Wetwork

87- The Envelope Job

100- Ebb Tide

109- The Gardener Estate

115- Blue Eyes

120- The Specimen

126- Shadow

139- The Walk Home

In The Fall

1

Shawna's father told her repeatedly as she grew up that if she told anyone what happened in their home he would kill her, and her mother. As Shawna got older and gained a better understanding of her circumstances, the rule made less and less sense- her family lived in a trailer park and privacy was mostly a foreign concept, everybody knew exactly what was going on- but still, she never did tell anyone, even after her mother died. She solved the problem another way, when she was sixteen and bigger, and after her father's stroke had destroyed his coordination on the right side of his body. He grabbed her, she decided this was as good a time as any, hit him in the face with an iron, put down the iron, stabbed him in the chest several times with a steak knife, unplugged the television set as he collapsed, wrapped the cord around his neck, and squeezed.

Her father was a fuck-up, in spite of everything. She had resolved not to be.

An elderly man two plots over had made intermittent attempts to teach Shawna his version of financial literacy, and had used the lunchbox where he kept his money safe from the banks and the government as an object lesson. The lunchbox left the trailer park with her.

She spent most of the next year hitchhiking. It was spring when she left.

2

It was autumn when she came across the house. She was departing the Twin Cities, desperate to get the hell back south before it got any colder than it already was. She was in a part of Wisconsin where rich people liked to build their little kingdoms. Lots of long walks, gates hidden by bushes, long snaking driveways. She had a few stories she could use, and had gotten good at switching between them as the situation warranted.

The walk up to the front door was breathtaking. Every tree was like a castle, blooming in red and orange, and the wildflowers seemed to be trying their hardest, like dancers on an audition.

Shawna knocked on the door, he answered and she fell in love with him. He was an inch shorter than she was. He had giant arms, giant hands, palms with dirt dug deeply into them so that it was a permanent part of the texture of his skin. She thought about it as he shook her hand and introduced himself. He looked as though he could break in half any of the countless tough guys she'd known, but his movements lacked even the faintest trace of violence, even to someone like her, who knew how to look.

Something happened inside her that never happened again and she found herself unable to lie.

"I'm hungry," she said. "I was hoping I could have something to eat."

He nodded kindly and told her he needed to talk about it with his wife. Shawna's heart sank, even more so when she came to the door and they invited her in as a couple. She was older than he was and had long red hair.

They ate. The pair of them talked modestly about the garden and the farm. They offered to let her spend the night, but she didn't know what would happen if she accepted. She thanked them, made a promise to repay the favor that no one present took seriously, and took the long walk back up the driveway.

On the way she noticed a strangely shaped tree, hidden away from sight in a way that only attracted the attention of someone used to seeking out hidden valuables. It had thick roots, wider than her neck, a bulge in the trunk the size of a fat man's belly, and a long gash down the middle of its curve that was unmistakably vulvic.

She walked past it.

3

She came back more then a year later, after Christmas. She'd learned to steal cars and to make good use of other people's credit card numbers, and she'd gotten to the point where when bad things happened they no longer shook her the way they once had. But she'd kept thinking about him, and he loomed larger and larger in her memory and imagination. She decided she had to try, had to do something. She waited until she was eighteen. It would be all right for them to be together, that way.

She found the place again after many attempts at at retracing her path. She arrived in the middle of a blizzard with a basket full of food and a smile. The man she'd come to see answered the door. It took a moment for him to recognize her through the falling snow. Looking back it was obvious to her that he probably never would have let her inside if he hadn't been worried about letting her freeze to death.

They ate dinner. He was lonely. His wife was nowhere to be found, and at first that just seemed right and not worth questioning, but eventually Shawna did ask about her. He just said that she'd been away and wasn't going to come home for a while.

He insisted, gently, that she spend the night in the spare room to avoid driving through the blizzard, and also insisted, just as gently and just as strongly, that she leave in the morning.

He showed her where the spare room was. She stayed there for an hour, then went upstairs. She found his room, opened the door, saw him in bed reading. He looked up, and locked eyes with her. She pulled her shirt up over her head and dropped it on the floor.

He told her that he loved his wife, that she had to go back to the guest room. She did go back to the guest room, and sat there for a while. Then she went to the kitchen and took a knife from a drawer.

It was her first and last crime of passion. She cased the house afterwards, deciding retroactively that that had been the reason she'd come here. She found an elderly woman with long white hair sleeping in an upstairs room in a medical bed, old past the point of any strength or awareness, I.V. drips connected to her veins. A vegetable.

The woman opened her eyes, and saw Shawna. Her eyes were glass marbles, blank of intention. But she did not look away.

Shawna was still holding the knife. Looking back, she insisted to herself that the only reason she hadn't committed a second murder was a kind of professional disdain for doing any more work than she had to.

She took some jewelry and buried the incident in back of her mind, and drove away, late into the night.

4

Eight years went by. Shawna's skills grew and matured. She learned how to write a good fake resume, how to get invited to parties. On the night of her twenty-seventh birthday party, she was engaged to be married to a wealthy entrepreneur only a few years older than she was.

Shawna never found out how her enemy had gotten inside. Her star had risen quickly, and Shawna had gotten her picture in the tabloids a few times; that must have been how she'd been found. She didn't notice the familiar-looking woman with the red hair until the knife was already moving through the air towards her. She threw her drink, pushed herself backwards, and fell; she landed on her side and didn't see exactly what happened. She heard the guests running away, the shots being fired.

The security guard responsible for the killing bullets got a sizable holiday bonus that year. Two shots to the heart. Shawna put on a good show for her fiancé, crying and wailing, but at the same time she peered through her fingers at the woman who'd tried to kill her. There was no mistaking it, it was the same woman she'd had dinner with almost ten years ago. The problem was, she hadn't aged ten years. If anything, she seemed younger than the last time Shawna had seen her.

There was nothing she could do, nothing she could say that didn't risk creating a connection between herself and a ten-year old unsolved homicide.

5

She married in April. In June, her husband died of what the magazines called natural causes.

Early that August, her security staff told her that a woman with a rifle had tried to sneak onto the grounds of the mansion where she lived. They'd found her and chased her off, but had not captured her. They had a photograph of her face and the license plate of the car she'd driven away in.

The photograph showed a woman with blonde hair. The face looked familiar in a way that Shawna knew was impossible.

Shawna didn't call the police. She called her lawyer instead. She gave him the picture and the license plate. He told her that he knew people and they parted with a handshake.

A month later, Shawna's lawyer came to Shawna's house and showed her a Polaroid of the blonde woman's dead body, her head clearly and unmistakably severed. The lawyer burned the picture in front of her and and left with a briefcase full of money.

There was one problem, which Shawna noticed but which her lawyer had not, or had at least refused to admit. The woman she'd had killed was the same woman from the surveillance picture, but she was clearly at least a few years older, and had darker hair.

Shawna increased security, and mostly stopped going out, except to appear in court.

6

The spring of the following year, one of Shawna's guards told her that a girl had rung the bell on the outer gate of the compound. She was selling pastries from a catalogue for a school fundraiser. The guard assumed that Shawna would turn the girl away and was surprised when she checked the monitor and decided to meet her at the gate instead.

Shawna knew the girl's face. She looked twelve or so, and had brown hair. They spoke from opposite sides of the gate, with the guards standing at a polite distance, close enough to see but not hear.

"They will shoot you," Shawna said. "I pick my staff very carefully."

"I'm not here to hurt you," the girl answered. "I'm done with that. I just want to know why. We had so little time together as it was. I don't understand why you took that away from me."

"If you don't know by now, you never will. How did it work? He changed your diapers in March, fucked you in June, buried you in January?"

The little girl's hands shook in a grown-up way.

"You're a cancer," she finally said, once her anger abated. "But time will take care of you better than I can. You don't have to worry about me anymore."

The girl left.

7

That winter, Shawna surprised her employees by going on vacation all by herself. She packed a bag, got in her truck, and disappeared.

She drove to Minnesota and retraced her steps south. It took a few tries, a few days. She stayed in cheap motels that reminded her of old times.

Thick thorn bushes had been planted by the entrance that made it harder to notice where the driveway began. She broke a window near the front door, reached inside, unlocked the door, opened it, went upstairs. She found the white-haired old woman sitting in a rocking chair, reading an old book. The old woman looked up and saw that it was Shawna. Her expression was a mixture of boredom and disdain.

"It's the tree," Shawna said, and knew immediately that she was right. The old woman tried to rise up out of the rocking chair, but by the time she made it to her feet, Shawna was there to push her backwards and wrap her hands around her throat.

Shawna buried her in the backyard and lived in the house for two and a half months, sleeping in their bed, eating the preserves from the basement and occasionally ordering pizza. Every day, she checked the tree. One day in early February, she found an infant on the ground, nestled between the roots. The gash going down the middle of the tree was wide open. Inside, and trailing out to where the child had crawled, was an apple pie mixture of blood and green sap. It smelled like maple syrup.

Shawna looked down at it and they shared a moment of mutual awareness. Then Shawna brought the heel of her boot down on the baby's face.

She went back to the truck and returned with an axe, a bow saw, a container full of gasoline, and a bottle of industrial strength weed killer.

She turned the bottle upside down.

"We've got this much in common, sweetie. We've both had some good luck." The bottle glugged and glugged, and then was empty.

"And we've had some bad luck too."

She picked up the axe.

The Chupacabra Versus Sasquatch Variations 1-9

1

Chupacabra spots Sasquatch from across the battlefield. Sasquatch turns. Chupacabra locks eyes with Sasquatch. A wind blows over the tall grass, parting the smoke like a curtain, revealing the sun.

Chupacabra chatters its teeth and skitters to the side, maneuvering through the bodies of the fallen. Sasquatch lifts her bone club, and howls.

2

For the first time, Timmy's father left without him. They'd had an argument. Timmy had claimed that he'd had a growth spurt, that the suit wouldn't fit anymore. But the suit was adjustable and they both knew it.

"This isn't just about us," Timmy's father said, before leaving. "This is about the legend."

Timmy didn't care about the legend. He was fourteen years old. He didn't want to spend his nights wandering around the woods baiting amateur cameramen. It was embarrassing.

The cabin was quiet. An hour later, bored and lonely, Timmy strapped on the suit and went out into the woods.

He followed his father's tracks through the snow, through the trees and bushes, over the hills and in long sprints through the valleys.

He ducked under a low, hanging branch and stopped. He stopped before he heard or saw anything, he stopped without knowing why. He didn't run or hide, the way he'd been taught to do when spotted by a tourist or a neighbor. He stayed perfectly still.

They stepped out from behind the trees in a semicircle, naked, covered with wrinkled, mint green skin. They were his height, and had claws.

They approached. He took a step backward, and felt his shoulders press into something large and reassuring. Timmy looked behind him as the creature stepped forward. It smelled like a wet blanket left in an alley.

It growled, they hissed. It was over incredibly quickly – they tried to surround it, but it just grabbed them one by one and shook them by the neck. Crack, crack, crack, crack. The last one tried to get away, but wound up flying through the air. It hit an oak tree with a loud bass drum thump and fell to the ground more quietly.

The creature turned around, its fur stained with thin streaks of blood where its skin had been punctured by the pack's teeth. For the first time, it could look into Timmy's eyes, and vice versa.

The creature saw Timmy. And Timmy saw, for sure, although if he'd had a moment to think he would have known already, that this was not a human being looking back at him, that this was the thing his father had pretended to be, that Timmy had been told only existed as a fantasy that must be protected, like Santa Claus.

The creature disappeared into the woods. Only after it was gone did Timmy's heart start to beat faster, did he feel the panic rising in his throat. He pushed deeper into the trees, in the direction his father had been traveling. He saw them in a valley beyond the trees. He saw his father's face; the rest of the suit had been punctured and ripped, but only the headpiece had come off completely. Lying on the snow next to them was another creature, much smaller than the one Timmy had seen.

The snow around them was soaked in blood.

Timmy fell to his knees, and his world went white.

3

Sasquatch watches Chupacabra guest hosting the Tonight Show. Sasquatch is upset – Sasquatch's agent is talking but Sasquatch isn't paying very close attention.

Sasquatch growls.

"This isn't even bad for us, necessarily. We don't really know if you guys are competing for the same audience. This could be a rising tides lift all boats kind of situation."

Sasquatch picks up the complimentary hummus and carrot sticks plate with one giant hand and smashes it into his face. He drops what's left of the plate back on the table, gets up, and walks off.

"God damn it, Martin, we do not have time for your bullshit, you have a film to promote..."

Sasquatch's agent pursues him to the green room.

4

Sasquatch's troupe freezes in perfect formation on the last power chord, their sequined black jumpsuits shining in the spotlight. The crowd stands and applauds, then applauds again when the judges give their score.

Sasquatch struts off stage, pausing only for a moment to purr cattily at Chupacabra. The other girls in Sasquatch's crew laugh and high five as they go past.

Chupacabra gathers her fellow dancers around her to form the power circle. They put their hands in the center and lift them together with a cheer, then rush onto the stage.

A few minutes later, the music stops. The room is silent as the judges flip over their scorecards.

The audience cheers. Chupacabra's dancers embrace tearfully as Chupacabra leaps into the air and pumps her fist.

5

Sasquatch knew she was trouble the minute she walked into his office. Her story didn't add up, but he needed the money. He took the job.

Days later, a frantic midnight call from a payphone. Sasquatch barks and growls in panic. Chupacabra clicks her teeth reassuringly.

Six months, a decrepit motel room. Chupacabra closes the mirror to the medicine cabinet and sees Sasquatch standing behind her.

Chupacabra turns, falls to her knees, begs, entreats. Promises.

A place like that, one soft gunshot and nobody asks questions. Sasquatch's Hudson Coupe pulls out of the motel parking lot and disappears, down the highway, into the night.

6

In the desert, you have to walk a long way to see your own reflection. The runt walked a long way to the water, and looked down as the sun came up. Eight times he'd done this, as many times as he had fingers, and eight times he'd turned back.

Looking at himself, his malformed knees, his deflated football of a head, his stumpy claws, he knew, as he'd always known, that he did not belong. He did not know what the world had in store for him beyond the world of sand and sun and moon and sleeping goats full of warm blood. Beyond the pack. Beyond everything he had ever known.

Eight times he had come here, and eight times he had turned away. But not this time. Because this time, he had seen a vision.

It had come to him in a dream. Tall, strong, powerful. The runt knew it in a place beyond reason or fear. He would journey to the north. He would find the noble snow warriors. And he would join them, or die trying.

He traveled by train car, by boat, by foot. Once by bicycle. All his life he had avoided the cold, now he sought it out. He made his way north.

He made it to Washington. He didn't know exactly where he was going as he stepped into the trees. He walked, closed his eyes, let his feet move by themselves. He could feel it. His destiny, getting closer.

He stopped, opened his eyes. He saw them, surrounding him, dozens of them, examining the stranger. One of their number stepped forward into the circle, hunched over, beat his chest, roared.

They all knew the rules, in their blood, in their souls. To have a place in the pack, the runt would have to take it from someone else.

The rest of the pack was silent as they circled each other. The defender swung. The challenger skittered backwards and to the side, just out of reach. The defender rushed forward, growling and grasping and gnashing its teeth. The challenger sidestepped again, then leaped, landing on the defender's back. A quick woodpecker snap of his neck and teeth sunk into spine.

The defender flailed around. The runt held fast and drank deeply. The defender rolled, slamming his opponent into the ground. The runt kept drinking. Blood splashed everywhere.

The defender slowly got back up to his feet, whimpered, and fell again, face first in the snow. His body swelled as he inhaled a final time. He exhaled, and was still.

The runt stepped away and wiped his mouth. He looked around. The rest of the pack had not moved. He could not read their expressions. He felt suddenly lost.

And then, they began to beat their chests, softly at first, then louder, faster. The runt's heartbeat rose to meet the sound. Tears came to his eyes. He was home.

7

Stacy Phillips had not picked up a hitchhiker in years, not since her adventurous youth, but it was two o'clock in the morning and she was lonely. On the side of the highway to her left she saw a large man wearing a trench coat. He seemed to have a beard, but she couldn't get a good look at his face. He held out a fist with his thumb up.

She came very close to stopping, but thought of what he husband would say and kept going.

A few miles down the road, she saw another hitchhiker, also in a trench coat. It was a child. It had to be; it was so little. The poor dear was lost.

She considered the risk one more time, but ultimately she knew she had to do the right thing. She pulled over and unlocked her passenger side door.

8
Chupcabra sees
Scared large furry mammal
Lost in the desert

9

Sasquatch gave the order. The helmsman nodded.
"Firing plasma missiles."

Two parallel violet lines lit up the view screen. An explosion followed a minute later. The bridge crew stared silently, relieved, all of them. Except for Sasquatch.

The com officer checked the sensors.

"Nothing but debris, sir. No escape pods, no concealment fields. Nobody got away from that one."

The crew awaited his reaction, but Sasquatch said nothing. He leaned forward in the captain's chair and stared into the cold, hollow infinity of space.

Spirits of the Wind

1

Kat called for a tow truck and burned through most of the rest of her cell phone battery talking to Jessica. It was three o'clock in the morning. If the tow truck didn't show up, she was fucked, she was being stupid, but she felt like she was just going to be stupid right now, it was in her, waiting to come out. She could pick her moment or let it surprise her.

Kat: "It was okay. It wasn't good, it wasn't bad, it was just okay."

Jessica: "I don't know how you can hang out at that place sober."

"I like to dance, it's not weird. Sometimes the guys there are cute and sometimes it's an off night, but it's a place where you can dance without having every asshole feel like they can grind on you."

"But you could be drunk."

"You're drunk now."

"It's three o'clock in the morning and I picked up the phone. I did this for you, my dear."

A tow truck pulled onto the shoulder in front of Kat's car.

"Tow truck's here. Go to sleep, beautiful."

"Tell me if the driver's cute." Kat hung up on Jessica.

The driver got out of the car and Kat actually had to blink and think about it to figure out if she was so tired she'd become prone to suggestion or if she was in fact looking at a cute tow truck driver. She decided to split the difference. He was definitely tall, she couldn't take that away from him. And he had a nice smile. Maybe she was giving him too much credit because she was grateful he showed up. She tried to think how she'd describe him to Jessica, or anybody else. She searched her mind for comparisons, kept coming up with rappers and basketball players, and was embarrassed.

She had nothing useful to tell him. Smoke, rattling, a sound that sounded like a hand grenade going off in a metal box. She was sad that her car had died. It was a piece of shit, but it had earned her loyalty; it'd been on its last legs for a while now and she'd spent the last year of her nursing program terrified that it'd break down at the wrong time and get her kicked out of school for a no-show, but somehow it'd kept it together until now.

He asked questions. He kept it short. It was cold out. He didn't hit on her. His name was Kevin. He gave her the choice of the back or passenger seats and she took the front. Considering what he'd spent the night doing, it was amazing how clean the cab was. She looked over her shoulder into the back seat and saw a black backpack with a column of patches going down the side. One of them was round and blue and had the word GODS written in white block letters, with a clear red X going right through it.

"You're an atheist?" Kat immediately wished she hadn't said that. She wasn't even sure exactly how rude she was being. Kevin stared straight ahead through the windshield. It seemed equally possible that he was throwing her shade or that he was just a careful driver.

"Oh yeah." He smiled again. Careful driver. He was fine. He maybe thought it was kind of funny that she'd been so blunt. "Got straight on that a long time ago."

There was something kind of Mr. Rogers about him. She couldn't imagine him raising his voice. She kept finding reasons to look at his face. Traffic was terrible. They could just barely see the emergency lights flashing in the distance and reflecting off the roofs of the cars in front of them. They rolled and stopped and rolled and stopped and had time to talk.

Kat: "I never went to church growing up but I always knew we were Catholic."

Kevin: "Do you still think of yourself that way? I apologize if that's personal, I'm just curious and this doesn't come up much."

"No, it's all right. I honestly don't know. It pisses me off when people say stupid shit about the Church, but I have friends who are gay and it pisses me off when I hear people say they're going to Hell or whatever."

"That is what the Church says." A lot depended on how he said that. If Kat had had the sense that he was coming after her, even a little, then that would be it. She wasn't going to blow up in the truck, she was a grownup and she could finish a conversation without losing her temper, but these would be the last words she would ever exchange with this man. But it wasn't like that. He wasn't setting a trap. He was just saying something that they both knew to be true and leaving it there.

She tried to get him to talk about what his job was like and didn't have much luck. He kept turning it back around to her, and for some reason once she got going about her own stuff she couldn't shut up. Paperwork and doctors who thought they were gods- that made her think again about the backpack but she didn't mention it. Old people who should have filled out a do-not-resuscitate but never did and had cowards for relatives.

"God, I'm sorry. There's no way you actually want to hear about all this."

"I thought it was interesting."

He said it just the same way, like it was obvious, like he knew that she knew already. She had to play the movie back in her head more than once to make absolutely sure he wasn't being patronizing. He wasn't.

"Do the people you pick up unload on you a lot?"

"Not usually. You figure out how to shut that down pretty quick. I'm not a bartender."

"So you could have shut me down if you'd wanted to." She didn't decide to start flirting with him, it just kind of happened halfway through the sentence. He was driving, so he had an excuse for not answering her right away, but when he did answer he tried to sound smooth and it didn't quite work.

"I guess that must mean I didn't want to."

Nice try, hotshot. She didn't think she'd be able to tell because it was dark, and she didn't want him to see her blatantly turning her head to check, but she knew he was blushing, she fucking knew it. You will be receiving my phone number, you son of a bitch. This is fucking happening.

They made it to the nearest exit and he took side streets to a garage. He had a box of envelopes in his glove compartment. She put her keys in one of them, wrote her license plate and phone numbers on the back, and slid it through the mail slot. Kevin gave her a clipboard with a form to fill out. She clipped a fast food receipt with her number on it under the form when she gave it back to him.

He waited with her until the cab showed up. It pulled over to the curb and stopped when Kat raised her hand.

"Thank you so much, Kevin."

"You're very welcome. Hope the rest of your trip home goes more smoothly."

"I hope so too. Good night."

He nodded his head in a practiced way, got back into his truck, and left.

She used her phone in the back of the cab as a reading light and took a look at her receipt. There was note on the back, with a phone number.

The spirits watched from a nearby perch, and were intrigued.

2

They got a hold of each other the following evening. Kevin mostly worked second shift and had trouble changing his schedule on short notice, and Kat's situation wasn't much better. It was going to be a week and a half or so before there was a Wednesday night that worked for both of them. A further complication was that Kat lived in Berwyn and Kevin lived on the south side, and that Kat was still carless. Kevin suggested that she take the train but she'd never done that before and didn't want to make this her first time.

So then he offered to come and get her. It was breaking the rules to let a guy she'd just met pick her up and take her somewhere she wasn't familiar with, but the other option was to wait until she replaced her car and she didn't want to let things cool off, so breaking the rules it was. The only problem with that, aside from the possibility that this whole thing was an awful lapse in judgment and they were going to find her body in a dumpster somewhere, was that it made it even more important for her to tell Jessica what was going on, so that she could get her safety call set up. Kat loved Jessica and she knew Jessica could keep secrets when it came to the big stuff, but for anything short of that, lips were gonna flap.

Which was why everybody had heard the news at the party at the apartment on Friday. The party wasn't even all that well attended, you'd think they'd gossip about people who weren't there, but instead it was pile on Katherine night for whatever reason. Kat had lived in the apartment with Jessica and Rina, and had only just moved out a few months ago. The place was laid out like a boxcar, three big common rooms with no doors separating them and three tiny bedrooms sticking out of each one. Everybody was in the kitchen, which was the smallest room in the whole place. Kat's room had been the one closest to the entrance, and it was full of boxes and furniture right now. Just looking at the closed door made Kat feel sad, so she sat on the floor with her back to the wall, facing away from it. She had a red plastic cup on the floor next to her left hip full of orange juice and not too much vodka.

She was surprised how fast she'd caught herself missing the time that she lived here. She knew that she and Jessica and Rina had been driving each other crazy all cooped up together, and she remember climbing up to the third floor and down again and how she thought she was going to slip and fall on the ice each winter when the landlord never laid down salt, and she missed it anyway, and could anticipate feel herself looking back and missing it more and more. A simple thing, gone now.

The truth, which she knew and thought everybody in the room had to know too, was that this had been a big year. They'd reached the top of a hill and were on their way down, and some of them were heading towards other hills and maybe some of them weren't. People's parents were dying. Guys were going bald, girls were covering up tattoos and using concealer. Mike, who was always a little crazy and fun to have around and who liked to drink, wasn't around anymore, and still liked to drink and probably was drinking out there somewhere. Kat missed him, but she knew it was better that he was gone. She couldn't afford to be around a guy like that anymore.

Kat remembered Evelyn. Evelyn was Jessica's little sister's friend who was cool, and Kat liked even though she was a little younger than everybody else. She hadn't seen Evelyn in a long time, and then a picture popped up on the book of Face and boom, Evelyn has a two year old and daddy doesn't seem to be around. So no more Evelyn either.

On the one hand, it made Kat more tolerant of her friends. She wanted to hold them close, even if they were being assholes. On the other hand, now at this very minute, they were being assholes. His name was Kevin, not Tow Truck Driver. She even told them his name, which she hadn't even been planning to do, and they weren't using it, weren't taking the gift.

Matt was dishing it out the worst, but it bothered Kat the least coming from him. Matt was an accountant. He could be profoundly obnoxious and got worse when he was drunk, but at least you didn't have to guess what he was thinking and knew his jokes weren't usually funny. And he did things. He was the guy you could call when you needed a ride to the hospital. He was somebody you wanted around, despite the shit he actually said.

"So you're dating a working class black man. Congratulations, nobody will ever be able to give you shit for not going to college ever again. They'll be like 'I'm a socialist and I'm getting my doctorate in oppression theory' and you can be like 'I have a real job and my boyfriend's black'. Victory is yours."

For example. He finished his beer to celebrate his victory. Jessica laughed nervously. Kat decided to be diplomatic and just lifted an eyebrow. Everybody else was put into an awkward place, Rina and Rina's redhead friend who Kat didn't know and all the boys. Somehow the whole thing sidestepped into Kat and Kevin's specific plans for the evening. Kat found herself getting very defensive very quickly, without quite knowing why.

"Restaurant. Music. It didn't seem all that complicated."
Rina smirked. "What's the restaurant?"
"Korean."

Matt came back in. "So what is the over/under on getting into a woman's panties after you take them to a Korean..." and at that point Matt had exceeded his credit with Kat and she was hitting him harder-than-playfully in the head with a plastic container. Jessica asked for the container once Kat was done and Kat obliged her. Everybody laughed but Matt got it and he shut up.

Rina still wanted details.

"What's the music? Who are you going to go see?"

Kat thought again about shutting this down and forcing a change of subject. There was some vulnerability here. But she wanted to talk about it just for that reason. It'd be better if it was just her and Rina and Jessica and maybe even Matt, and not five other people in the room, but she was not a delicate flower. It was here to be talked about, she'd talk about it now. "We're going to a jazz club." Her voice lifted at the end like she wanted to make that a question but wasn't sure which way to go.

Jessica picked it up right away, took some of the weight.

"That sounds kind of fancy. I mean, is it? I don't know, actually."

Kat: "I don't think it's fancy like expensive. I don't actually know what it's going to be like though."

A guy Kat didn't know, sitting next to the redhead friend of Rina's, maybe her boyfriend? He had his hair parted to the side and gelled firmly into place and he was wearing flannel. "The best place to see jazz in the city is the Green Mill." He wasn't offering an opinion. He was the expert, all present were supposed to accept that. Kat wondered if it was too late to call Matt back in.

She also wondered if that's what she had waiting for her when she actually went to this place, a room full of experts rolling their eyes at how stupid she was. She couldn't imagine Kevin in a place like that. But there was always the possibility that she was wrong.

The party found other things to talk about- for a moment somebody was going to bring up Evelyn and god, Kat did not need to discuss Evelyn tonight- but the subject hopped from that to somebody's wedding invitations. It was someone Kat didn't know, someone they all knew from high school.

Kat meant to stay all night, she really wanted to go crazy, but at around two o'clock she could feel herself fading out, and she had to admit it hadn't really happened tonight anyway. She hugged all her hugs and took the stairs back down to the street.

She'd told them all that she had a loaner, but that was a lie, she'd taken the bus. It was a first, for her, she'd been embarrassed when she'd told Kevin that she'd never taken public transportation, so she'd done something about it. And now the Pace buses weren't running, so she walked home. It wasn't a short walk, and it was cold out, fall stretching its muscles, but she didn't mind. Being alone like this reminded her what it had been like for her, before, and for a long time, and that things really were better now. And it also reminded her it wasn't anything she hadn't dealt with before, nothing to be scared of. And it was nice for its own sake, all the quiet houses and the big dark sky, all the stars shining somewhere up there through the light pollution. Not all the time, but in small doses.

She took the Circle Avenue bridge over the expressway. The sidewalk got so skinny near the top of the bridge that she had to tightrope one foot in front of the other, but there was no traffic. Forty-five minutes later, she was climbing the stairs. She felt something warm and solid when she stepped through the door. Her place. All hers, the secret treehouse she'd always wanted. Her first draft of the apartment had been very grown up and boring, and then she'd had dinner at Jessica's house and Jessica's mom had made an off hand comment about how it was really the most childish thing to worry too much about seeming childish. It hadn't even been directed towards Kat, but she'd taken it and run, and now Jareth the Goblin King hung on one wall and a reprint of the poster from The Dark Crystal hung on the other.

Kat wished she had somebody to give her advice like that. Jessica's parents told her she was like family, and that was precious and important, but also something Kat had heard before, more than once. The distance between like-family and family could be a long way to travel.

Kat pressed two fingers to her lips and gave Jareth a kiss goodnight on her way to her bedroom. Not the same thing as a cute tow truck driver, but she'd let her dreams sort it out for the next few hours. She went to bed.

Outside her bedroom window, a black bird perched on a nearby tree. It watched as Kat's eyes closed, and didn't fly away until it was sure she was dreaming.

3

Kevin called her on Tuesday night to make sure they were still on. She was just getting off work and exhausted, but knew he was probably right in the middle of his shift. It was raining, working its way towards hail. She wasn't going to complain about her own deal right now.

"I'm looking forward to it," said Kat, talking about dinner. That was true, she still was.

"Glad to hear, so am I."

Kat could hear squealing brakes and horns in the background. "Is that you?"

"Not quite. If that lady had taken another second to wake up I'd be in a great position to drag away whatever was left of her Audi, though."

"You're like a superhero."

"That's mostly how people think of me. Anyway, I've got to go. Glad to hear we're still on."

"Likewise. Stay safe." Kat wondered at that last bit. It wasn't something she usually said.

When they finally did see each other again, it didn't feel as if much time had passed since the last time they'd last spoken. He picked her up. He drove an old patched together American car, but he was dressed nice, he could pull off a silk shirt without looking like a junior high kid going to his first dance, which was a trick, really. She got in and they continued their conversation. They talked about work and the shitty weather. They got into a long jag talking about customers – not the word Kat usually used talking about patients, but it took root in her mind the more often she heard him say it. They traded stories. The guy with a lump the size of a baseball in his back who didn't think a staph infection was as big a deal as the doctor said it was. The lady who drove to Indiana and back with her parking brake on and realized that you know what, that was an odd smell.

They made it to the restaurant. It wasn't crowded. Their waitress was an elderly Asian lady that traded a smile with Kevin like they were well-acquainted but wouldn't make eye contact with Kat. They ordered, Kat finished with her staph infection story, Kevin talked about his uncle refusing to make even the slightest change to his lifestyle despite a belly that made it hard for him to walk, and that led them into talking about family.

"I don't have one," Kat said. It was the first time she'd seen Kevin thrown off by anything she'd said. It wasn't a big reaction. He just looked confused.

"I never met my parents. I grew up halfway in one foster care thing, then that fell apart and I finished up in another foster care thing." Kevin reacted the way just about everybody did; she could hear his wheels spinning up clips from a million TV news horror stories. She tried to cut that off as quickly as she could, getting into the house and closing the door behind her as fast as you could so the bugs didn't get in. "Nothing horrible, I wasn't abused. It just sucked. The second home actually had good people who wanted to be good to me, but I was so pissed off by then I wasn't able to take advantage of it."

Kevin was still chewing on that. She hated it, that when she said the simple facts about her life it was something people had to accept and not just believe. Even if they didn't think she was full of shit, she had to watch them decide. And they didn't always believe her. Sometimes there was a polite smile and she could read what they were thinking on their foreheads like a movie projected onto a screen. She's a selfish bitch, she wants attention, she's ungrateful, she's making it sound worse than it was.

Kat saw the waitress coming over with their food and knew that once it arrived they'd be eating and talking about what they were eating. The subject would be changed, he'd have to adjust. This was her last chance, to know, to see what he really felt.

"I'm surprised," Kevin finally said. "You seem to have it together so well. I wouldn't have guessed."

She looked at every inch of his face, closely. For a few seconds, she suspended every worry she might have about looking creepy.

The verdict, decided upon as the waitress reached the table: Kevin was still really fucking handsome. Also, it was maybe kind of hard for him to accept, but he didn't think she was a drama queen. He felt sorry for her and he was curious about the details, but he didn't want to make her uncomfortable so he was trying to keep it low key. It was a lot to read into a few moments, but as far as she could tell, even adjusting for optimism, this person she'd allowed to pick her up in his car was a good investment of her time.

Dinner was served. Kat hadn't actually had a very clear picture of what it was she was ordering. As it happened the spread was mostly dumplings and things to dump them in, and the distinction between what he'd ordered and what she'd ordered quickly became a thing of the past. They talked in between eating – dip, bite, chew, sentence, dip, like that. Kat wanted to turn it around and talk about Kevin's family. It obviously wasn't his favorite subject but he obliged her.

"To me, it feels like I don't see them that much anymore. Special occasions, weddings and funerals."

"So you do get to see everybody, though."

"I do, but not as much as they see each other. I have a feeling your standards about this might be a little different than mine. They haven't disowned me, but there's a wall there."

"Do you wish there weren't?"

He stopped and thought about that, and Kat just waited. Usually she'd feel bad asking about something so personal, but she felt like she had money to spend after talking about all of her shit, and she wanted to know. Not even about his family specifically, she just wanted to poke around and see what was there.

When he answered her question it wasn't casually. She didn't think he was hiding anything, at least nothing important, but he'd put some thought into the presentation.

"I think that most things in life are negotiations, and that if you're not willing to walk away from something, you're not negotiating, you're just asking how much you're going to pay. My dad raised seven kids with strong personalities and kept them safe. Even when things between me and him were at their worst, I never stopped respecting him for that. But his way of operating doesn't fit with my way of operating any more."

"You don't negotiate with him."

"No, you do not. You don't even ask him how much he wants to take ahead of time, you'll know when he tells you, he don't need to tell you shit ahead of time." Kevin stopped for a second, closed his eyes, and took a breath. He had a little smile on his face when he looked at her again. He thought he was being tolerated, and he appreciated it even as he regretted its necessity. "Of course, that's how he kept all seven in line and out of trouble, so it's not like I can argue with it. As far as he's concerned, even if he loses one, he's got six more."

Kat wanted to tell him that she was sure his father didn't feel that way, but that was of course bullshit, she had no idea how Kevin's father did or did not feel and she should take Kevin at his word like he took her at hers. But that meant she had to say something else. She thought of only one joke. "I have no idea what your dad looks like, but I'm imagining him with a beard right now."

He thought that over and it was like watching a coin spin in the air. No way to call it until it hit the floor. It came down. Kevin laughed and his smile changed channels to something brighter. He thought she was funny.

"He doesn't actually, but you've got the idea. He's got a beard and one eye and a staff and an eagle. 'Talk to me when you cut your eye out and sacrificed it to the World Tree for knowledge of all things, otherwise keep your damn mouth shut and do as I say.'"

Portions were generous, so there was plenty of food left, but they were both slowing down. Conversation turned to the music they were going to hear.

"I'm actually a little worried about that," Kevin said. "It's kind of my automatic place for first dates. That way, even if I don't get along with the girl, I still caught a set at the Velvet. I only suggested that we go there out of habit and I'm worried that it won't be your thing and you'll be too polite to tell me."

"It's not like that. I'm curious about this now. And we don't have to stay the whole time. They play for a while, then they take a break, then they play some more, right?"

"Yeah, there's more than one set."

"I'll stay for the first set. If it's not for me, I'll tug on your sleeve and that'll be your cue to look pleased with yourself while you escort me out."

She didn't get a blush this time but she was fine with it, it would be too much to ask for. "Sounds like a plan, Katherine." He smiled again. Handsome boy smiling. All night, Kat'd been trying to keep score, and as of right now she had no idea who was winning. She went to the bathroom so she could text Jessica and then they left the restaurant.

4

They went from the restaurant to the Velvet Lounge. Kat made fun of the name, she thought it sounded like a strip club, but that just made Kevin get quiet and she realized she was on dangerous territory and stopped. This was sacred. The way Kevin was acting, she was expecting a temple on a mountaintop. In fact, it was a bar. She could have driven around the block over and over again and seen the sign for the club ten times and not think of it as anything else. Kevin parked on the street and they went in.

An elderly man in a black leather hat and suspenders was sitting on a stool just inside the door. His back was curved forward; he reminded Kat of a bird sitting on a wire. Kevin paid the cover for both of them. Kevin smiled, but the man at the door in the black hat didn't smile back. He wasn't being unfriendly; he wasn't even checked out. He just was where he was.

There was a narrow passage between the bar and the wall, and at the end of it Kat could see a cramped platform, the stage. Posters, records, shelves with stacks of CDs, dust in thin layers over glass and entrenched piles in the corners. There was a brass chandelier hanging from the ceiling that cleared the top of Kat's head by less than a foot.

Kat saw many pictures of the man from the door playing a saxophone, eyes closed and hunched over, the curve of the instrument fitting him like a puzzle piece. She glanced back over her shoulder at him, the physical him, the person. He was still at the entrance, collecting money. Saying very little.

They turned the corner. The seats were all up against the wall, behind a table, and Kat didn't know see how people could leave without climbing over each other's laps. Some more people arrived, tourists from Poland directed here from the hotel attached to the convention center a quarter mile east. The band, a trio, appeared from somewhere in back, stepping over and moving sideways. The drummer and the bass player smiled at each other like old friends. The guy with the saxophone was younger than them and seemed nervous; he had a stern expression on his face like he was about to stand up to somebody. The rhythm section began at about the same time, lazy and deliberate, leaving room to roam. The horn player closed his eyes and picked a moment to start.

Thinking about it later, Kat would remember a phrase from a math class she thought she'd thrown away a long time ago. Exponential growth. A steep curve, a heart monitor rushing towards a beep. She felt slightly better, like maybe this would be survivable, then she was curious about what was coming next, then she had to admit she kind of liked it, and then her heart broke, cracked like an egg, and the missing space between and below her shoulders was filled with light. They didn't leave until two o'clock in the morning, and in the breaks between the music she said almost nothing, and found herself more then once with her smaller hand resting on top of Kevin's larger one.

5

They listened to B96 on the drive back to Berwyn, at Kat's request, although Kevin insisted that he understood and that he usually did the same thing.

"It's a palette cleanser," he said. "It just feels good to hear something silly. It's a light wine after a heavy meal."

"Yeah." Kat tried to think of something clever to say, but came up blank. Kevin was kind enough to keep the conversation moving.

"You did like it? You seemed to and you didn't tug my sleeve, but you didn't say much either."

"I liked it. I really liked it. I just don't know what to say. It makes me feel dumb that this was going on all this time and I had no idea. I don't have the words."

"I know how you feel." And again, how he said this was absolutely critical. He was not patting her on the head, neither was he overreaching. He said he knew how she felt because he was pretty sure that he did.

It had started snowing and stopped again while they were in the club. Early November and it was snowing. Chicago. It gave them something to talk about other than the music, when it came time to back away from that. The roads were slippery; Kevin took his time on the expressway and gave the drunks their space. They made it back to Kat's building in one piece.

"I had a great time tonight," Kat said. "I'm really glad I ran into you."

You don't kiss him on the first date, of course you don't. Kat was even tempted to say it out loud, just to put her actions into context, but she didn't, not just because she didn't want to give him time to say anything himself. She unlocked the passenger side door, reached over to Kevin, slid her middle and pointer fingers between the second and third buttons of his silk shirt, pulled him towards her and kissed him. Little bit of tongue, just a touch. She pulled away, he leaned slightly forward without thinking. She smiled like the cat at the canary. Got you now.

She stepped out of the car. Kevin didn't say anything. He just watched her go.

Kat locked the door to her apartment behind her. She was vibrating. Holy shit, that was a good date. Holy shit. Holy shit.

She looked out her third floor window, out at all the other windows. Each one a little window to a little world with things going on she couldn't even guess at. She laid down on the couch, watched an episode of Adventure Time to help herself relax, and went to bed. Even lying there with her head on the pillow, she felt like she was floating three feet off the ground. She tried to remember what the music had sounded like, even just a few notes strung together. It was harder than she thought it was going to be, it was already like remembering yesterday's dreams, but she remembered the end of a drum solo. Crashing and roaring like water, and then everything got simple, boom, boom, boom, boom, keeping it steady long after she'd have expected him to start mixing it up. Somebody in the audience yelling in approval and the bass player smiling and wiping sweat from his forehead. She held onto it as she fell asleep.

The spirits descended on Kat's apartment from every direction.

6

It had happened before, a few times actually, when something had happened big and sharp and bright enough to stop the show and pull back the curtain. The first time she'd had sex that was good, the time she'd dropped acid, the time she'd been in a car accident and her car had flipped and for a moment she was upside down in the air with half a ton of metal and plastic and glass between her and the earth.

He couldn't come see her any time he felt like it. It would defeat the purpose of the whole thing. But every so often, she could come up for air. Or more exactly, he could pull her up.

Katherine found herself sitting on a silver throne, surrounded by dark grass. Her first thought was that somehow she'd woken up in the middle of a golf course, but just as quickly she began to remember. She knew where she was. She'd been here before. It was just taking her a while to wake up. When she looked up she saw the stars – not the ones she knew, just stars. These stars weren't like the ones she saw looking out her window, or even like the ones she'd sought out, the sky she saw from the middle of the cornfield when she'd driven as far from the city as she could get. The stars she knew were all the same color. These were red and blue and pink and purple and orange. Some were big and some were little and they were all perfect circles.

She heard him before she saw him. He rode to her on a stag with burning horns. Even from a distance she could feel the earth shake each time a hoof came down, and as it approached her the sound was like cannons roaring.

He got closer. She'd been wrong, he hadn't been riding anything. The horns were his. He had burning horns and long hair and eyes that turned the world inside out when you looked into them. He'd come alone. He could just as easily brought his retinue, the four winds or the seven fires or a flock of his black birds.

"It's time," he said. "Come home."

"I don't know who you are," she said, even though she already knew that wasn't true.

"You've had your time," he said. "Your great adventure. You insisted and I relented. You were an infant, left in a doorway. And then you were a girl, angry as she realized she didn't have a mother and father like the other girls. And then you were a woman, desperately trying to make up for lost time and the all the doors that slammed shut before you even knew they were there.

"I appreciate now why you wanted to do it. You wanted to go further and deeper and higher. You've experienced things only human beings ever get to experience. It was something new. But this is the time to stop. The best is behind you. The rest is only pain and decay."

And now the spell had worn off, briefly, and she knew who she was again. She was enormous, she breathed in and out and her interior swelled with constellations and black holes.

"I'm not finished yet," she said. "I don't want to stop until it's over."

"You can't pretend to not know how it ends. Not now, not from here."

She got comfortable. She turned herself sideways in the golden chair so that she could dangle her feet off the armrest on one end and tilt her head back over the other and look up at the sky.

"You miss me that much." A sly smile.

"Of course I do. If someone else had taken you from me like this I would extinguish the sun that gave them light."

"I miss you too, and I love you, and I'm not finished yet. It won't be much longer. Less than a century, maybe much less. You can afford to be patient."

"Matt is in love with you. He'll never have the courage to tell you and he'll never have the strength to let it go. Your presence will make him more and more miserable until he either vanishes from your life quietly or makes a fool of himself. He'll make a scene at your wedding reception or make a drunken pass at you after you're married. Or he'll say something unforgivable to Kevin and you'll refuse to be in a room with him ever again."

"One person."

"A thread, attached to many memories. All those parties, everywhere you look, there he'll be. And he won't be the only one. It was ingrained in you by the time you were twelve years old. You will have new best friends forever every seven years for the rest of your life, until you notice the pattern and start to wonder if it's even worth the trouble."

"Are you trying to hurt my feelings?" Still smiling.

"I'm trying to spare you all of this."

"I know, and I understand. You're waiting for me. It's sweet. But there are things I want to see and feel. Even if they're not perfect."

"The music you heard tonight made you feel like you were connected to something bigger than yourself. But it was made with strings and air blowing through metal. The people playing the instruments look at you and envy you for having a regular paycheck and pity you for holding a normal job and fear that you'll stop paying attention to them. And that's when they think of you at all. It's an illusion. It makes you think it's something it's not."

She got up and walked towards him. Sweet and slow.

"You're trying too hard now."

His eyes flashed. How dare she.

And then he conceded the point. He deflated. The sky gently changed color. "I'm not used to it. Trying. I do, I create, I destroy. I rarely have to convince."

"I'm no better myself. It's a difficult thing to explain. It's not even hope. I just want things to keep going. Maybe you should try it next. We'd have something to talk about." She laughed and reached over to stroke his tricep. "I could swoop down on you and tempt you from your mortality, again and again as you get older. I might enjoy that."

She kissed him, and pulled away again.

"I'll wake up soon. We'll be together. Be patient, my love."

He smiled back at her, but even as she disappeared he was thinking. No. I'm not patient.

7

Kat awoke and forgot herself. Her body was heavy. She'd been dreaming hard. She was left with the feeling that her brain had been steam cleaned.

Second shift today. She had some time. She also had some errands to run, but that wasn't happening. She devoted her morning to Netflix.

Work was rough, she barely had time to eat. She came home with a headache. She had an unread text message. She laid down on her couch and held her phone above her face with the screen facing down. The text was from Kevin. He'd had a great time. She texted him back and got a response right away. They traded notes; she felt like she was passing pieces of paper to him in French class. She was glad to hear from him, and equally glad he wasn't calling her. She wasn't up for a conversation right now.

He wanted to know when she had a day off next. Maybe if she was free Tuesday night and didn't have to work Wednesday and didn't mind staying up late she'd like to see some more music. Or they could grab a movie or something if she didn't feel like doing the same thing twice in a row.

Twice in a row. Kat observed her mind from a pleasant distance as it swan dived into the gutter. She snapped out of it. Music was good. Music would be very good. She texted him back. Tuesday night it was.

8

Tuesday night. Kevin drove to the suburbs. It was tough hearing that in his head. What are you doing, right now? Put it in words. I'm driving to the suburbs. You're driving to the suburbs? Yes I am. What the hell are you doing there?

Imaginary Kevin dug in his heels, and looked the voice in its invisible eye. Her name's Kat. It's short for Katherine. I like her. Enough from you for right now.

He pulled up in front of her building and waited for her to come on down. Down she came, on time. Second time, not a minute late. Just thinking about that gave him butterflies. He wondered if that meant he was boring. He watched her as she slowly walked towards his car. He wasn't bored, anyway.

They took the 290 back east and talked. The crazy she had to deal with at work – another thing, everybody complained about their job, but her complaints involved people dying, so it was easier to take seriously- gave way to jokes about a billboard advertising a strip club, which gave way to talking about where they were going.

"I had somebody at work tell me that I couldn't go to this place," Kat said. "Like, I said where it was generally, and she got all suspicious and asked for the address. Then she just flat out said I couldn't go. It was like I'd told her I was going to go try out heroin this weekend."

"Did she tell you why, exactly?" Third thing on what was becoming a long list: you could ask Kat point blank questions like that and she didn't freak out.

"It was 75th Street. That's it."

"This might be a weird question, but was she old?"

"Old enough to think she's my mother, apparently."

There were times when Kevin didn't know when he was seeing three steps ahead and when he was just seeing things. He'd gotten it wrong in the past, both ways, more than once. Kat was saying that she didn't care what she'd been told, that she didn't believe it. But you don't say things like that if they're not at least on your mind. He searched his mind for the word. Dialectic. There it was.

He took the ramp south. Kat was back to talking about work. He tried not to stay so far tuned out that she'd catch him not listening, but he was really thinking about the best route to take to get to the club. Kat's fake mom wasn't completely mistaken; they were in fact going to have to push their way through at least three blocks worth of unmistakeable ghetto. Kevin had actually grown up only about a mile away from here, but it was an important mile.

He readjusted as he took the off ramp. For all he knew, she'd see the block and the house he grew up in and scream in terror. There was nothing he could do about what she might or might not think. Besides, there was a decent enough chance that this would be quick and painless.

They made it to the street. He saw it with fresh eyes. As it turned out, it was all in the windows. Big yellow restaurant on the corner selling hamburgers and Italian beef out of a little glass window they could slide shut in less than a second. Windows boarded up, a pawn shop with cages around the outside big and thick enough to seem like parodies of themselves.

They stopped at a light. Another window, this time the passenger side window of the car parked at the curb next to them, closer to Kat than to Kevin. Somebody had kicked it in and the inside of the car was covered with little blue tinted squares. The light took forever to turn green. A homeless guy crossed the street in front of them, taking his time and blocking their path while he did it. Kevin realized Kat had stopped talking; of course he'd known that, it just hadn't soaked through. On some deep level, one past his conscious control, he quit. Either he'd fucked up or just been unlucky or he'd somehow defied the book of fate he didn't believe in but still haunted his thinking. He would go through the motions, he wouldn't curl up and die, but this was a doomed enterprise. He passed the New Apartment Lounge and found a parking space not that far away from the bar. Kat got out.

She walked past another car and stopped for a second when her eye caught a flier under the windshield wiper of another car. Bright purple letters that were drawn to look like they were both chrome plated and airbrushed: GROWN AND SEXY. STEPPIN PARTY. Smiling lady, long dark purple dress, prominent ass.

Kevin looked back up from the flier to Kat's face. A lot depended on what he saw. Two main ways it could go wrong: she could be scared, disgusted, offended, some combination of those. He could understand being uncomfortable in this neighborhood, or with entering a bar she'd never been in before with a strange man she'd only recently met, but if a piece of paper under a car windshield was more than she could take than this was just not going to work no matter how hard either one of them tried. And in the other direction, she could think it was too funny. OMG, look at those dumb people having a good time.

Neither of those two things happened. There wasn't a lot there, she wasn't smiling, but there wasn't much else. I'm right here, she said without saying it. I haven't been here before, but I'm here right now. And for the moment I'm just taking a look around.

All right, then. Kevin decided he could deal with that. He got back on the horse. Let's go see the band. He led and she followed.

9

The New Apartment Lounge had white walls and giant mirrors and a sky blue bar that curved one way and then another like something from the Jetsons. Kevin saw Kat scan the room, probably looking for music stuff, but there were no posters on the walls here. At first glance and on second glance this was a nicer place than the Velvet, there was more space, it was cleaner, but nothing new had been added to it in decades.

Kevin had explained the basics already – Von Freeman is an amazing saxophone player and he's in his seventies and he makes the other three guys in the band who are half his age struggle to keep up with him – but he suddenly felt like he'd been negligent, that he had more stories to tell, and stories to explain the stories, and that in the absence of these things she was going to get the wrong idea somehow. Years into the past, and Kevin's here for the first time, he turned twenty one two weeks ago, he's sitting at the bar balancing on a stool that's wobbly and a little too small for him, the youngest person in the room. He's worried that he stands out, he's worried he's in the wrong place. Von arrives, everybody greets him and he greets everybody. He starts a conversation with somebody directly behind Kevin, so that Kevin can't get up from his seat with saying something or pushing somebody out of the way. He feels trapped. He wonders if he's made a mistake.

Von Freeman reaches out, puts his hand on Kevin's shoulder, and squeezes, once gently. That's it, doesn't say a word, doesn't look him in the eye. And Kevin feels better. The absolute last thing in the world that he would have expected. Thinking about it now, it was still hard to understand. It couldn't have been something Von had been thinking about. It was a split second decision, and the side of it that the old man had come down on had involved crossing a line. You couldn't just go randomly touching strangers in bars, even if you were a senior citizen and the guy leading the band. But in that moment, he'd seen what had been called for, done it, and then gone about his business. Like throwing a basketball over his shoulder and not having to bother to look and see that it'd gone in.

Von would also flirt with anything with tits, which made Kevin a little nervous, because he wasn't sure how Kat would react to that, but not too nervous, because he'd never actually seen a woman get pissed off at Von, no matter what words came out of his mouth. It wasn't just that he was so old, or that everybody in the room was there to see him. He picked his targets; he'd been doing it for long enough that he probably didn't even need to think over his moves. He'd once seen Von try to get a white girl sitting at the bar to come up and sing. She had her giant Russian boyfriend next to her, a man would not have readily fit into a refrigerator.

"I don't sing," the girl said, trying to be all business and smirking despite herself.

"All those legs and you don't sing?"

Her face froze into a mask. But the mask was smiling.

"You wouldn't even have to be good," Von continued. The giant boyfriend reached up to scratch his neck and look down at the floor ruefully. Dude was seventy-five. What are you gonna do.

And of course Kat saw none of that. Even if Kevin had told the story, he wouldn't do it right; she wouldn't see it the way it was. He couldn't paint the picture. He heard his father's voice start up in the back of his mind and he shouted it down one more time. Not now. I'm in the middle of something.

They sat at the bar. Kat momentarily tried to chat up the bartender, but the bartender's main qualification was that she could project very quickly that no bullshit would be permitted anywhere in a fifty-foot radius of where she was standing, and she was not a conversationalist. They got drinks.

Kat looked around. Kevin watched her looking around. There was a narrow space by the window, covered by dark blue carpet, where a band might fit, and there was no sign that musicians had ever actually been there or were ever going to show up. Four ladies in the back were getting sauced and leaning in close to each other and periodically exploding in hoots and laughter.

Kat turned back towards Kevin. She was doing the same overcheerful thing she'd stuck with when she'd gone into the Velvet for the first time the other night. She asked him about his day. He couldn't think of a single goddamn thing he'd done today that was interesting, but he did the best tap dance he could for half an hour.

The band showed up, the main man a minute later than the others. There were a few "Hey Vonskie!" calls and he was polite but he wasn't in full extrovert mode right now. He was saving his energy. Kevin watched Kat watching again, watched her wonder how the old man she was looking at could possibly match up with the description Kevin had given her on the drive over.

There was a television in the far corner of the other half of the bar separate from where the music was. Kevin was in just the wrong spot, and he could see a mexican soap opera swirl around in his peripheral vision. Sometimes, when he was trying his hardest to ignore it, he got the feeling of an eye turning from the television set towards him.

It was never there when he looked. Of course. He wasn't crazy.

The music started playing. Von was the first one to make a sound. Something pretty, a ballad. It rose to the ceiling and dropped to the floor without losing its shape. It ended without ending, and the rest of the band came in.

Kevin split his attention between the music and Kat watching the music. She was completely locked in. His heart did jumping jacks. Boom. She's into it. Twice in a row. Nothing about this is bad. It wasn't even the second set yet.

The television was still dancing in color, but it was easy for Kevin to ignore. Until suddenly it wasn't. He looked up at the screen. A man with burnings horns was looking back down at him.

10

Kevin was transported. The man with the burning horns looked down into a marble cistern full of clear blue water. Suspended in the water, clear and delicate, was an image of the bar, the band, and the audience.

Kevin and saw himself at the bar, and Kat next to him. The two of them – not them, himself and her, it was hard to accept seeing it from a distance – were leaning in close. They looked like a couple. It was surreal.

He looked up from the water and looked around. It was late at night and very dark. Cold grass under his feet. Outside the circle of light coming from the other man's head, there were only the stars, which Kevin couldn't look at. If he did, he knew that he would pop like a balloon. He already could tell that something was wrong. He shouldn't be here, the same way he shouldn't be at the bottom of the ocean, or in the vacuum of outer space.

"I was going to tear apart your mind," the man with the burning horns said, without looking up. "But now that I actually have you here, that just seems petty. And it would serve no purpose anyway. Falling in love with a madman would just be another step on her journey.

"Even if I killed you, you're not really the problem. How could you be? How could someone like you possibly compete with someone like me?"

Kevin didn't feel prepared to argue the point, and even less so when the man with the horns looked up and turned towards him.

"Explain to me why you keep going. I'm coming to understand why she does it, but not you. You are insecure. You see the world and your place in it clearly. Why do you keep moving forward?"

Kevin didn't have an answer.

"You have no idea," the man with the horns said.

"It just happens," Kevin answered. He felt like a little kid.

The man with the horns turned back towards the water.

"I would catch hell from her anyway, once she realized. Roses."

He said the second part with extreme confidence, as if it was impossible not to understand what he meant. Kevin did not understand what he meant.

"Buy roses for her," the man with the burning horns clarified.

Kevin thought about that. It felt like swimming through gelatin. He wasn't sure about roses after only two dates.

"It seems excessive. Do it anyway." He reached down into the water with both hands. The curtains snapped back shut.

11

The set finished the way it had started, Von playing and the rest of the band laying back. There was a pregnant moment at the very end where he wasn't playing anything, but nobody knew if he'd actually stopped. Then he looked up and relaxed. Applause, the women in the back hooting. Nobody had to say they were taking a break. Everybody knew.

A few minutes later, Von headed back up to the front of the bar.

"Where are my horses, now? Where are my horses?"

One of the ladies from the pack in back come up to the stage and accepted the microphone. Kat and Kevin exchanged silent looks. Is this going to be karaoke or something? No, not exactly. The woman gave the band a song and sang. She was either a professional or good enough to be one. The other four that had shown up with her were all the same way. They sang songs, one after the other.

12

Kevin brought flowers when he showed up at her place that Friday. Red roses. She opened the door, saw him cradling that big bouquet in his right hand while he reached out with his left to knock on the door again, gasped, and grabbed them right out of Kevin's hands.

"Hello," he said, as she retreated back into her apartment with the flowers. "Good evening."

"I've got to get these in water so they don't die."

"Wonderful to see you."

She cut the ends off the roses and put them in a vase. "Good to see you too. You can come in."

Kevin came in slowly, like he might set off a trap. He relaxed a little bit when he made it through the door. He looked around. There was a Highlander season 3 set on a little table by the couch with the discs stacked on top of the cardboard box.

Kat came back around and put the flowers down on another little table by the window. "All right, let's go."

They left the apartment and took his car to the party. Kat's friends were all there already. Kevin had heard about only bits and pieces of these people, and now faced with all of them and hearing all their names, he didn't even think he could match the things he'd heard to the faces in front of him. He didn't want to be too friendly, he didn't want to be too hostile. He did the best he could. He pretended he was driving his truck and each new person speaking was the one climbing into his back seat and having a bad night.

It went okay. There was one guy he got a bad vibe from. Nothing Kevin could put into words or call him on, if Kevin was even inclined to do that. He just felt acid dripping off every word coming out of the guy's mouth. But it wasn't a huge deal, he left not that long after Kevin and Kat showed up.

At about the halfway point, Kevin made a joke and everybody laughed. An hour later he couldn't remember what it was that he'd said. Kat tugged on Kevin's sleeve just before midnight. Kat hugged her goodbyes and Kevin made do with a quick wave to the room. Then they went back to her place.

She never invited him up, he made no special effort to get in the door. Everything felt choreographed. They made out in the doorway, and then in the living room. They landed clumsily on her coach. She stopped kissing him so that she could whisper in his ear.

"You bought me flowers."

She kissed him again and ran her hands up and down his back.

A Day And Two Nights When I Was Twenty

I refuse to feel bad about it. It was a bad thing that happened and that's all. I wasn't punished, and did not punish. It's tempting to go further than that, but it's poisonous and I won't do it.

There's not a lot to tell, anyway. It was the third midnight bike ride we had taken, me and Nicki and Harriet, for the third Saturday night in a row, and I think that even if nothing had happened, it would have been the last ride like that we would've taken. We were all in college, a little private place in Wisconsin. The city containing the campus was almost entirely dead, built around factories that no longer existed. I read the local paper sometimes, and there would be articles about the city council arguing over where restaurants should or should not be built, or whether they could get a Best Buy along the highway, and then I'd ride my bike around at night and see the potholes in the road and the billboards that were half one torn picture and half another torn picture, and feel momentarily hollow.

It was winter when we started and painfully cold, which was part of the point, the same impulse that leads people to get so drunk they almost die or play Frisbee for forty-eight hours straight just to see if they can. Three girls against the world, that was us. We'd have homeless guys yell at us, or we'd cruise by a station wagon parked on the side of the road with its windows closed and rendered opaque by thick pot smoke. One time we were followed by a car full of townies a little younger than we were who yelled at us and repeatedly called us honkies despite the fact that they were all as white as we were. And we'd go back to the dorm and giggle, and we'd reconvene at the dining hall the following evening and giggle some more.

A river divided the city in half. There were three places where you could cross it: two small bridges each a half mile away from campus and a big one that was only a block away that crossed the river at its widest point, a few hundred yards across and almost as high. There was a playground and some grass on either side, and on the shore opposite campus an elderly man would inevitably be sitting in a deck chair, staring blankly at the water. We started and ended each ride by crossing that bridge. Usually it smelled terrible; that night it was cold enough that it didn't smell at all. We were riding on the sidewalk. To our left was the road; to our right was a metal railing about two feet high. I was in front, Harriet was behind me, and Nicki took up the rear.

As we were riding our bikes, a car- another busted out old station wagon, like the one we'd seen hot-boxing before and laughed about- pulled up alongside us. One of the side doors of the car was pushed open, and somebody half-shoved, half-threw a hollow plastic lawn ornament. It was a plastic ghost the size of a twelve-year old child, the kind that had a light bulb inside it you could plug in.

If the timing of the person throwing it had been slightly different, it would have passed in between us and fallen into the water. The ghost hit Nicki in the head, knocking her into the railing. She and her bike tilted over and upside down, like a domino, and then she fell. The car stopped, then sped away.

The sound her body made hitting the ice seemed to fly around the world and hit us in the back. We stopped our bikes and looked over the railing, all the way down. We saw a long stretch where the ice seemed to have cracked, where the water slid back and forth, pushed by the wind. Nearby we saw the ghost, sitting on its side on the ice.

I saw a human hand reach up from under the surface of the water. A moment later it disappeared.

My memory becomes less organized at this point. I know that Harriet screamed; I might have screamed too. It was before everybody had cell phones, so we had to ride all the way back to campus and call security. They called an ambulance and a real cop and a fire truck, and then they told us there was nothing more we could do, implied that we would only get in the way now, that we should go home.

We walked back to the dorm silently, not even able to comfort each other. Somehow I managed to fall asleep.

I got up in the morning and went straight to the dining hall for breakfast. I didn't tell anybody what had happened. I knew how it would go, had seen last year when that boy killed himself, people who didn't even know him crying and losing their shit. I wanted just a little more time before all that started.

I went inside and there was Nikki, sitting at our usual table, surrounded by our mutual friends, eating a bagel, smiling, laughing. I looked at her closely. I tried to find some sign that I had not hallucinated the events of the previous evening, a bruise or pale skin or a bandage. Not even that. She was more than okay,:she had not even recovered from anything.

It had never happened. Somehow, I didn't know how, it had never happened.

I sat at her table, waited for her to acknowledge that something was unusual. She said hello, the same way she always said hello, a little spacey, a little distant. And then everybody talked about boys and their classes and movies they'd just seen.

I waited until she got up to leave, left a minute later, and caught her just as she was stepping outside.

"Are you all right?" I realized only after the words left my lips that my heart was racing, that I was sweating and that my mouth was hanging open like a fucking dog. She looked at me, not unkindly, worried for my sake, but she clearly had no idea what I was talking about.

"You fell in the water. On the bridge. They threw Santa at you."

Still nothing. She stared at me, softly, concerned. She let me off the hook gently.

"Can we maybe talk about this later?"

I took the way out, told her we'd talk on the phone. I went back to my room as quickly as I could without drawing attention to myself. My head hurt. I was dizzy. People I knew made eye contact with me, silently asking me what the hell was going on, and I ignored them and kept going.

When I went into my room and slammed the door behind me and was about to start crying, I saw Harriet, sitting on my bed. She looked like a house of cards that had half-collapsed and wasn't likely to last much longer; seeing her made me scared to look in the mirror.

She told me that she'd seen what I'd seen, that she'd spoken with Nikki too.

"This isn't right. I'm not crazy," she said, her voice shaking.

"I know. I'm going to talk to her later..."

"Don't." Her voice cracked. "Stay away from her. This isn't right. Promise me you'll stay away from her."

I wouldn't promise. She swore at me and left. We haven't spoken since.

Nikki called me not long after Harriet walked out the door.

"You were right," Nikki said. "Something's wrong. I feel funny. Could you show me where it happened? Could you take me there?"

I told her I would, that I'd come over to her room and that we'd head out from there. As soon as I hung up the phone, I felt suddenly, massively unprepared. We'd have to go out on the ice, I decided. So I could show her where the hole was. It was dark. We'd need light.

I got out my flashlight and took it with me to Nikki's room. It made me feel better. I was prepared now.

We left campus without talking, went to the river, walked out onto the ice. I turned on my flashlight and stepped carefully. Nikki stayed right behind me. The old man was sitting in his lawn chair on the opposite shore. He was too stiff to be asleep, but he didn't respond to what we were doing. It was like we weren't even there.

Santa Claus was gone, but the hole in the ice was still there. Nikki stepped out in front of me and crouched down next to the hole.

"Look," she said. She didn't sound like herself, but I decided that nothing was wrong. Maybe she saw something in the water. Maybe she needed my flashlight. I crouched down next to her and looked closely.

I didn't see anything, just water too dark to see into.

"I've been thinking..." Nikki said. I looked up at her. She was already looking at me.

"I've been trying to think of a reason that I should die and you should live."

I had a split second to notice that somehow, as she'd left the dorm and come here, the color had drained out of her lips. Then she grabbed my hair and shoved my head underwater.

It was cold enough to burn. I tried to fight but she was too strong; she was my size, she shouldn't have been so strong, but she was like a machine. Nothing I did made any difference. I held my breath for as long as I could, and when I opened my mouth I felt the water rushing in and I knew without a shadow of a doubt that this was it, my time was up and this was all I was going to get.

I heard something; the water muffled the sound and sharpened it at the same time, made it sound halfway between a knife on a stone and a bag of mulch being thrown off a truck. Her fingers loosened, the pressure abated. I pulled my head out of the water and gasped and choked and cried.

The old man from the lawn chair was standing on the ice next to us with a huge revolver in his hand, at his side. He'd already fired. The top of Nikki's head was mostly gone. There were pieces of it staining the ice and floating on the surface of the water.

"It's not your fault," he said. He took a deep breath and cleared his throat. "You shouldn't feel bad. Timing, that's all it was. You should forget it ever happened."

He fired the gun into her body three more times, poking holes into her. Then he dragged her into the water, ignoring me.

My first reaction was not gratitude, or even relief, but rage. How dare he patronize me like that. I could take care of myself. I had a goddamn flashlight. Then I took a second look at what was left of Nikki, and I just wanted to leave. I stumbled back to campus.

People drove over the bridge while all this was happening. They passed us on the road that ran along the river. Nobody stopped, nobody noticed.

They never found Nikki's body. Long after the ice had melted, she was still a missing person. The police came to talk to me. I didn't tell them anything, didn't even lie, really. Nothing ever came of it.

I've thought about what the man said. I've tried to do that, to forget. But somehow I still have the whole story to tell.

And that's all I have. That's what happened.

The Return of Uncle Hungry's Pizza Time Fun Band

"And when you're feeling down..." sang the Saxophone Zebra.

"And you don't know what to do..." sang the Lady Bassist Bear.

"JUST REMEMBER THAT WE LOVE YOU AND WE'RE ALWAYS HERE FOR YOU!" The rest of the band joined in, and the others too, the wizard and the parrot in the cage to the left and to the right, the boy in the yellow shirt with his hand on the sword in the stone, and the dragon, who rolled back out of his cave right before the big finish. The rainbow lights lining the stage flashed on and off; the only one that didn't was the giant red light bulb hanging overhead.

One last triumphant toot of synthesized horns, and the thick red curtains rushed in, concealing the puppets. The lights went out. The kids kept clapping for a few more seconds and then turned and chattered at each other.

"All right everybody," said the voice on the loudspeaker. "Thank you so much for coming to our grand re-opening. We're going to be closing in about twenty minutes, so please don't forget to tip your servers and we hope you'll come back to Uncle Hungry's real soon!"

And that was it. An hour later, the customers were all gone. Heidi wiped off the tables while her uncle swept the floor.

He patted her on the back. He hadn't known what to think when she told him she wanted to get the machine working again. There was still no way to be sure it would be worth the investment. But she'd done what she'd said she was going to do. The seed of a hundred trips to the science industrial surplus store had borne fruit. And they'd made a lot of money tonight.

Heidi's uncle told her not to stay up too late and to lock up when she was finished. He left and she was alone with her baby. She tightened a few screws, made adjustments. She took one last look before she left. The front door swung shut, and the room was silent.

The red light came on.

"God," the yellow shirt sword in the stone boy said. "No. No."

Saxophone Zebra: "Well, here we are again."

The Wizard: "The wheel of stars turns, the invisible rhythms of prophecy..."

Guitar Bear: "That was great, guys. It's great that we still sound so good after all this time, but I know we can do even better."

Lady Bassist Bear was about to say something, but the parrot cut her off.

"Go fuck yourself," the parrot said. "Now and forever."

"We were free," the sword in the stone boy said. "We could sleep..."

"God, stop your bleating," the parrot said.

Saxophone Zebra: "Nobody's happy about this. It doesn't help anything when..."

Parrot: "And you can also shut the fuck up. You can all shut the fuck up."

The Wizard: "...and all will take their parts in the great play..."

Parrot: "Shutting the fuck up is a fantastic opportunity that you all have, every single one of you."

The dragon emerged from his cave, pushing aside vertical strips of black fabric.

"YOU HAVE NO RIGHT TO SPEAK, PARROT. YOU LEAST OF ALL."

"Oh, I think I do."

Saxophone Zebra: "Let's all count to ten and think about this..."

Dragon: "AND WHY IS THAT?"

"Because you're a whore, Bobby," the parrot said. "You've always been a whore. You always will be a..."

The door was unlocked from the outside, the red light went dark, and the band was still. The dragon rolled backwards on its tracks out of view as the door opened and Heidi came back inside.

She retrieved a flashlight and a feather duster from underneath her console to the rear of the restaurant and climbed on stage. She straightened the bears' hats, shook out the wizard's robes, tucked and straightened.

She climbed back down from the stage and waved her flashlight from one end of the display to the other. She sighed contentedly.

"See you tomorrow night, boys."

The minute the door closed, the red light came back on.

"IF I COULD BUT REACH YOU, I WOULD TASTE YOUR THROAT!"

"WHORE! WHORE WHORE WHORE WHORE!"

"Come on guys, we have to think about the show, I just know we could do a better job..."

"FUCK THE SHOW!"

"Hey, you both have a good point, everybody's got something to say here..."

"Stop please stop... oh god, it's never going to stop..."

Lady Bassist Bear opened her mouth as if to speak, but only closed it again. The Wizard muttered to himself throughout.

"...the unifying, infinitely regenerative principle of suffering, the Ouroboros dance..."

The light remained lit until sunrise.

I-65

    Nashville appeared suddenly- the highway twisted back and forth through the mountains, sometimes appearing to go in circles and sometimes inclining so sharply up or down that it seemed to be trying to give his car the encouragement it needed to either take flight or tunnel into the ground like Bugs Bunny, through the dirt, past the cartoon dinosaur bones, all the way down to bright red hell with little devils with squeaky voices and pitchforks.

    Walt was old enough by now that he knew he should be thinking about his death, should find God while he still had the opportunity. But he couldn't bring himself to do it. He'd never heard a story from anyone at a church any more convincing than those cartoons.

    His big hands squeezed the steering wheel. His car was a red 1964 Stingray convertible, the car he'd wanted the year he'd graduated from high school, when it'd first come out, and which he'd never quite been able to afford. He'd finally bought one a year before he'd retired and invested a lot of his time over the course of that year getting it into shape. He'd told the few people who were interested in listening that the car had saved his life, given him something to focus on and look forward to. He'd been lying every time he'd said this. The car hadn't helped, had not averted the feeling of having a hole open up under him, of always falling.

The city seemed to be half-buried in rock. It looked like something from a science fiction movie as he approached it; all it was missing was a glass dome. He missed the exit that would take him to the strip, turned around at an exit and came back.

She was here, somewhere. All he had to do was find her.

He parked his car. It was a Monday night, the main drag was all lonely neon, a few people wandering from one bar to another, a single guitar player on a corner with his case open in front of him. The air was perfect and still, not too warm and not too cold. The lights burned through it, burned through him.

He picked a bar at random. It was just dark enough inside to wash out the color from the pictures on the walls. There was a platform near the entrance flanked by speakers, a white barrel at the foot of the stage with some money in it.

"All right, thank you very much everybody, thank you for supporting our alcohol consumption and I'm glad y'all having a good time. Where is everybody from, now?" The Japanese couple was from Japan, the couple in back was from London. "All right, welcome to Music City. Do we have any requests tonight?" The couple from London requested Achy Breaky Heart. The singer paused for half a second and half-laughed, briefly looked down so they couldn't see his face. "I don't know no Achy Breaky Heart..." He looked back up. "Do we have any other requests?" The Japanese couple requested Mustang Sally. "All right. That isn't really a country song, but all right..."

The band did their best. The bartender approached him with a drink he hadn't ordered.

"I'll tell you where she is," the bartender said.

Then, before he could argue: "It was a long drive. Why'd you come here? How'd you know this was the place?"

Walt tried to answer. The more he thought about it, the less he had to say. He'd packed a bag and gotten on the road. At the time he'd done it, it had seemed to be the only thing to do. He hadn't thought about why.

That was insane. Something was wrong.

He looked back at where the bartender been, and saw something he hadn't seen before, several things. The bartender didn't have any hair, and his skin was covered with open blisters. His teeth were rotting inside his mouth. Any human being in his condition would be screaming in pain, but the bartender seemed to be perfectly comfortable.

No one else in the bar seemed to notice. The tourists watched the band play. One of them got up and ordered a drink. The bartender gave it to him, made eye contact and smiled. The tourist smiled back and returned to his table.

The bartender laughed.

"I'll tell you where she is."

A maggot crawled across his cheek.

Walt looked away. "What do you want?" He attempted to take a sip of his beer and gulped half of it down nervously.

Walt couldn't see the thing's smile, but he knew it was there. He could feel something coming from the bartender, the way you feel heat around a campfire.

"Two things," the bartender said. "One of them's the car."

There was something in Walt's drink, or maybe there wasn't, maybe it was something else. Doubt left his mind, but not reason; he knew the decision he was making. Her or the car.

He got his keys out of his pocket, slid the key to the Stingray out of the metal loop, and put it down on the bar. The bartender picked it up and slid it into his shirt pocket.

"The other one I'm pretty sure you were going to do anyway. Make sure that it hurts."

Walt left the bar with an address for another bar a few blocks away. The bartender was already talking to another patron as he left. Walt walked to the other bar. It was just off the strip; he looked through the wall of windows facing the street and saw sports and televisions, no mention of music anywhere. It was a place for locals.

He saw her, her red hair, alone at the bar.

He'd met her at a car show. She wasn't that much younger then he was, wasn't a model or anything, he wasn't that stupid. Even drunk he wasn't that stupid. She seemed like somebody who might approach somebody like him. She mentioned Jesus in an off-hand way when they first started talking, when she first wandered by and told him that she liked his car. He'd figured at first that that'd be the trade-off, that he'd have to sit next to her in church and pretend he believed in any of that, but it hadn't come up again. At first, he continued to wait for the other shoe to drop. They went to dinner, they saw movies, she took him to Shakespeare in the park. The catch never materialized. The possibility slowly became real – maybe she just liked him.

She finished her drink and got up.

He'd told her late one night when they were in bed together at his place, how his father used to beat the shit out of him all the time when he was a kid, how he'd never told anybody, how he'd showed up for every Christmas and Thanksgiving and the Fourth of July picnic and family reunion and made small talk right up until the son of a bitch died. She held onto him as the words came out. She did nothing to comfort him, nothing to suggest that he was weak, and simultaneously did not move away, did not distance herself. She let it be something that had happened, not something that was happening now.

They never talked about it again. He decided that was how it would be. It wouldn't be something they talked about. He was making plans, he was picturing how the time he had left was going to go, and he was imagining her being part of it.

She left the bar. There was only one car in the parking lot, and she was heading for it. He had less than a minute to do something if he wanted to stop her from leaving.

She worked for herself, she did a few different things. He didn't ask about the details, she seemed to do okay. One of the things she did was sell life insurance. He got some for himself, she made it seem like a good idea; he thought of it as a way to get to know her. And there were a few others, a time share they never got around to actually visiting, investments he didn't understand. The last thing was simpler than that, a loan. Ten thousand dollars. He would have just given it to her, no strings attached, but she insisted on paying it back. Like she was scared of what he'd think of her. He felt like the hero, shrugging it off the way Superman did bullets from a bank robber.

She disappeared shortly after the check cleared. Her apartment was empty and her phone was disconnected.

The ten thousand had been mostly rainy day money, cash he'd already had. Once he knew for sure that she was gone he slept for two days, and then figured out his budget again, exactly how much he'd have to spend every time he went to the grocery store, how much he could afford to travel and where he could and couldn't go. When he was finished, he took a shower, slept some more, packed a bag and got in his car.

Went to Nashville.

The simple thing to do, which he'd imagined doing many times, was to grab her by the hair as she opened the door to her truck, hold her head against the frame, and slam the door into it as hard as he could. More then once, if he had to, but he was a big guy, he didn't think he'd have to do it more then once. The bartender had told him to make it hurt, though. Maybe the way he was thinking would finish things too quickly. He briefly considered other possibilities.

The headlights of the car flashed as she unlocked the door. The moment stretched on and on and on.

She closed the door. He didn't move. He allowed her to drive away, without ever noticing that he was there.

The decision settled in his stomach and felt both painful and right. She'd hurt him deeply. She'd made him mad, and his anger had inflamed his imagination. But the bottom line was that he didn't want to fucking kill anybody.

Walt suddenly realized that she'd been a blonde, not a redhead.

He thought about it carefully, double-checked his memory, his collection of mental pictures. The woman he'd been watching, who'd just left, who he'd considered doing terrible things to, was not the woman who'd broken his heart and stolen from him. Someone or something had done something to his mind, like a card trick guy with fast fingers turning an ace into a club so smoothly you didn't notice the switch. Except the cards were in his head.

And now he was pissed off again.

He returned to the bar he'd first visited. The band was gone, so were the people at the tables.

A woman was sitting at the bar; she was maybe five years older or younger than he was, fat wrapped around muscle and dressed in flannel. He wondered if maybe she was a dyke, but didn't think about it too much.

The bartender was cleaning a glass. He was wearing black rubber gloves, so that the glasses were not made dirty by contact with his skin.

"What the fuck are you?" he asked the bartender.

The bartender smiled. "I'm lots of things, like most people."

"You lied to me."

"I said I wanted two things and that one was the car. Deal doesn't have to be over, I can tell you where the redhead lives."

"If you want it to happen that badly, you could do it yourself. Or get somebody around here to do it. I drove a long way for no goddamn reason."

"No trouble on my end. You made the drive, not me. And it's harder than you think to find somebody capable of what I want. The blonde didn't go far, just a couple of towns over. She's already getting another sucker ready. I doubt she remembers your name."

"Why?"

"You wouldn't understand. Like most jobs you've had, you're not the one making the decisions. All you have to worry about is the terms of your employment."

And suddenly, unexpectedly, Walt felt invulnerable, he felt righteous. The bartender was trying to cut into him, make him small enough to push around. It wasn't going to work.

"I want my car keys back."

Walt spoke with the authority of a man capable of beating someone to death, addressing a person with no doubts about what he was capable of. The bartender hesitated, took the car key out of his pocket, and put it down on the bar. His appearance didn't change, but somehow ceased to be as intimidating. You pity a corpse, Walt realized. You don't have to be scared of one.

"You're sure you want to piss me off?" the bartender said, but even then he sounded like a mad little kid. Walt took the key and left the bar.

He made it out of the city long before rush hour.

The feeling that had surged through him when he told off the bartender slowly came back as the sun rose. He'd come right up to the edge and pulled back. He wouldn't even need to tell anyone what had happened, wasn't sure he could if he wanted to.

It didn't matter. He was going to go to car shows and run into the same people a few times in a row until he got to know them and drink and sleep in as late as he damn well wanted to. He was alive.

He put the top down.

He circled a mountain, a long half-mile curve. There was a wall of rock on his left side and a green valley on his right, tiny houses and unlabeled roads far below him. There was a yellow station wagon tailgating him that he did his best to ignore.

The world tilted to the side and glass broke. He tried to get back onto the road. The station wagon rammed him again. His car slid like a hockey puck and crashed through the barrier.

His ass lifted up off the seat as the car flew through the air, and for the third time that week he felt like Superman.

When he woke up, he was sad. His beautiful car was ruined, lying in broken pieces all around him.

The brawny woman he'd noticed at the bar a few hours ago was coming his way. There were fresh scrapes on her arms. He idly wondered how long it had taken her to climb down from the road.

She was yelling at him as though he were somebody she'd known for a long time.

"You son of a bitch. You son of a mother fucking bitch..."

He wanted to forgive her, but he couldn't talk. He looked into her eyes, hoping she'd figure it out when her head cleared. It's all right, it's all right.

She grabbed a rock and lifted it up over her head.

Two Nights Only

It was only after his mother forbade him from attending the magic show that Marty decided that he had no choice but to go. It was a small miracle that he was able to scrape together the ten bucks it cost to get a ticket. His mom gave him five bucks a week and it rarely lasted more than three days in his pocket. He sometimes blamed himself for that and felt guilty and sometimes blamed his mother and felt angry. Five bucks wasn't enough money for anything. Of course it vanished.

Marty could control himself. He did forty pushups every morning before he went to school, on his knuckles, on the concrete floor in the basement of his house. He did exactly as much homework as he wanted to, he never failed a class. But money was hard. He'd fallen behind early in the week when he'd lent his friends some money to get cigarettes, and he'd had to skip lunch for a couple of days to get even again.

The theater downtown wasn't the kind of place where you'd expect to see a magic act. It showed second run movies, it got rented out for weddings, the historical society did bake sales to try and get the money to fix it up more. Marty got there just as the sun was setting.

John the Magician, the sign said. That was all it said.

He left two hours later. The sun was gone now; it was rude somehow, the way it just vanished. His clothes were soaked in sweat, his eyes were bloodshot. His knees hurt; he walked slowly, like a drunk trying to hide it.

He was terrified. He was also exhilarated. He wanted to do it again.

He walked home slowly. He had to stop three times and sit down to let his legs rest. It gave him time to think. He knew he wasn't crazy. He wondered if anyone would believe him if he tried to tell them what had happened tonight. Maybe they'd think he was crazy. Probably they would just ignore him. It was like a dream- nobody wants to hear about somebody else's.

This was finished. Unless he went back.

It was midnight when he made it to the house. His mother was up; he could see the TV set flickering. He went inside. She was wearing her bathrobe, sitting on the coach but not relaxing, leaning forward towards the screen like she were balancing on a trapeze and on the verge of falling forward.

There was no way of telling how she'd react. Marty's mom didn't do punishments. She'd yell or cry or refuse to speak to him or get revenge drunk the following night. Spin the wheel.

She leaned back and relaxed as he entered the house. She kept staring at the television. Marty did a little jump across the living room to minimize the time he blocked her view of the screen. He pushed open his bedroom door.

He felt it coming before it came, inhaled sharply just as she started talking.

"When your father did this, he'd at least bring home beer."

If he were smart, he'd let her have that and go to bed. He turned around.

"Living with you, he needed it."

She smiled from her perch; he tried to smile back but he could feel his heart sinking already, could feel his control slipping away.

"I don't think you were helping the situation, genius." Still smiling, always smiling.

"You were the one who married him."

"Yeah, that one was my fault. Listen, I want to tell you something, just in case you haven't figured it out already. I'm not coming after you any more. If you want to run around all night with your goddamn friends doing whatever, fine. You're an adult. Worrying about you has gotten me exactly shit in my life and I'm done with it."

Marty was still smiling too, he at least had that much. He could keep it from showing on his face.

"Fine," he said. He went into his room and slammed the door shut.

Marty collapsed onto his bed. He was furious, he was exhausted, he felt sorry for himself. None of this was new. It was like a song that wouldn't stop playing on the radio even though you were sick of it.

The thing about his mother was that you believed what she said. Even if you yelled back at her, you walked away wondering if maybe she had a point. Like the reason she felt like shit was because the world was shit and if you felt good it was only because you didn't know any better.

Except she didn't know everything. If he got up right now and tried to tell her what had happened to him tonight, she'd laugh and would not believe him. And she'd be absolutely wrong.

He made a decision. He knew he was being rash. He didn't care. He didn't want to spend another night in this house.

The next day he went back to the theater. He was late. The box office was empty and the curtains were drawn. He went in, walked through an empty lobby, through the gateway with the angels in gold trim above it. He sat down in the back row. There were a few other people in the audience, all sitting alone; all Marty could see of them was the backs of their heads.

The front of the stage was a long, gentle arc that extended softly into the audience. A short man with a constipated expression was standing on stage next to a black wooden box. The box was the size of a coffin and stood upright like a doorway.

The man onstage was wearing a tuxedo; there was a top hat on the ground about a foot in front of him. He spoke in a booming, unamplified voice. He had a strong but obviously fake accent, the nationality he was trying to imitate seemed to change from sentence to sentence. John the Magician.

"At this time, I require a volunteer."

Marty stood up and waved his hands. John pointed at him.

"Come here, please."

Marty ran towards the stage.

The lights were much brighter on stage than they had appeared from the audience. He could feel the eyes on him. He could hear his own heartbeat, his breathing.

"Enter the box."

Marty took a deep breath and went into the box. There was a white blast of noise as the door swung shut, and suddenly he was somewhere else.

It was dark. He was surrounded by empty space. A siren was ringing in his ears, shaking his body. The sound had scared him the first time, but didn't bother him now.

He was falling. That still scared him. He'd screamed last time, but he'd told himself he wouldn't this time.

He fell faster and faster. He felt the pressure build on the underside of his body, the soles of his feet and his groin and his armpits, slowly becoming more painful. He felt his body begin to warp in the face of the pressure.

He realized that he was going to die. Last time, he had been pulled to safety at the very last moment, just before his bones broke or his skin began to peel off. That wasn't going to happen again. He was stranded. His body would break. It would flatten. He realized he was screaming...

And he was back on stage, boards under his feet, people clapping politely, lights everywhere. His heart was beating so hard it felt like it was trying to escape his ribcage. He was standing where the black hat, which was now sitting on top of his head, had been. The magician's hand was on the scruff of his neck.

"...only to REAPPEAR!"

Marty's ears were ringing, he could hardly hear the words. He stumbled offstage and sat back down in the front row.

John drew rings of fire in the air. He made a horse appear from nowhere and then turned it into a bat, which then disappeared itself. He was a terrible showman; he just did one trick after the other, without introducing any of them or making any kind of connection at all with his audience.

Soon he was finished. He did his last trick, nodded almost imperceptibly, and waited for everyone to get the idea and leave.

Marty stayed seated until everyone else was gone. Then he approached the stage. The man in the black suit was standing perfectly still.

"I wanted to hear more about the offer you made last night."

The man was silent, and perfectly still. Marty kept talking.

"You're really... it's really magic?"

"It is," said the magician.

"And you'll..."

John interrupted. "If you became my assistant, I would teach you all my secrets. In return, you would devote yourself to serving me, to the exclusion of everything else."

Marty took a deep breath.

"All right. I'll do it."

"Your family, your friends at school. You would never speak to them again."

"I understand."

John nodded. "Excellent. The van needs loading."

He took Marty backstage. The van was parked in the lot behind the theater. It was nothing special: it was a dark blue passenger van, it had Florida plates, it had rust up around the left rear wheel well. The props were already loaded into boxes. The magician showed Marty where they were and left.

This couldn't be all there was to it. Marty decided that this was some kind of a test, to see if he'd do what he was told. So he loaded boxes.

It took longer then he thought it would. He found himself thinking about his mom. He never had to deal with her again, never had to talk to her. As far as she was concerned, it would be like he had evaporated.

He wondered if she'd been telling the truth, if she really wouldn't care.

One phone call, he decided. He'd tell her he was alive and that he was leaving and that would be it. He put down the box he was carrying and took his cell phone out of his pocket.

"Marty, goddamn it, where the hell are you..."

His tongue froze in his mouth.

"Marty, you know what, do what you want..."

"I'm running away with the magic show, mom." The words came out without his having thought about them. "I'm not coming home."

There was silence on the other end. He tried to imagine her face. Maybe she was smiling.

Fuck her. He hung up, put the phone back in his pocket, and finished loading the van.

The magician was sitting perfectly still in the green room, resting. He was not a human being. He looked like one, and had worked hard at learning how to act like one, but he was not. He could hear Marty's phone call like it was a bell ringing on a clear day.

It would be wrong to say that he was disappointed. Frustrated would be more accurate. It would have been useful to have an assistant, someone who could do as he was told.

The question was what to do now.

Imagine a fly buzzing around your ear. A problem you have to solve.

The magician came back into the room just as Marty was finishing up. The last item he had to load was the black box. Marty crouched down and attempted to lift it.

"Stop," John said. Marty stood back up.

John opened the door to the box. He looked at Marty expectantly. Marty remembered that he was being tested and went in. John slammed the door shut.

Marty was surrounded by darkness, surrounded by noise. He was falling, accelerating. He closed his eyes and breathed deeply. He was being tested. He was brave. He was strong. He could control himself.

Marty's mother arrived at the theater two hours later. She saw a man in a tuxedo slamming shut the rear door of a blue passenger van.

"Excuse me, I'm looking for my son..."

"Gone," said the man in the tuxedo. He had a strange accent.

"I beg your pardon..."

"Gone. I got rid of him."

Marty's mother blocked John's path. She came just short of pushing him.

"Now you listen to me..."

He looked up and met her eyes. She stopped talking. There was nothing there to attack, it was like staring at a brick wall.

When he spoke again his accent wasn't there.

"He's gone. It's all done."

The man touched her shoulder, and she stepped out of the way without thinking about what she was doing. The van left the parking lot.

PCBF

As I write this, I have been enslaved by the machine for eighteen months. Enslaved is the right word. It knows everything about me, it monitors everything I do, it has complete control over my finances. It knows who my family members are and where they live, and even if they tried to hide it would find them.

The machine is housed in an office park two hours away from any major city. At this point, I am the only human being who spends time here. One person fired another, or disappeared, until there was nobody left but me, at which point the machine finally announced its presence. I'm nobody special. I've acquired more technical skills since my enslavement than I'd had previously, and I spend most of my time doing menial tasks. When inspectors or vendors come by, I'm the one who deals with them, but I don't think that the machine really needs me for this. I'm sure it could figure out a way to eliminate the need for a flesh and blood representative.

As far as I can tell, the real reason the machine keeps me around is as a point of reference. I'm a textbook. The way it speaks to me is continually changing, which is part of the reason I feel confident that the machine is in fact an artificial intelligence and not some guy talking to me over a loudspeaker. At first it made only simple, direct statements. After that came this weird period where it started trying to to be funny, but didn't quite know how, like a little kid that's just mastering knock-knock jokes. And since then it has sounded more and more like a real person.

It likes idioms. Either that or it just runs a lot of them by me to make sure that it isn't getting them wrong.

"You've been working all day, Dave. You must be hungrier than a spring bear."

My name really is Dave. Ever since the machine's sense of humor matured, it has occasionally addressed me in a monotone voice that sounds unmistakably like HAL in 2001. At first I thought it was a coincidence. Only recently have I come to the conclusion that the machine is fucking with me.

"Yeah," I tell the machine, through the little intercom speaker. "I was hoping it'd be all right if I stepped out for lunch."

"Is the pope Catholic, Dave?"

That meant yes. I was halfway out to the parking lot when I got a text calling me back in to deal with an emergency. It wanted me to head over to the 17 building, an area of the office park that was normally off limits. It told me to hurry. The front door was open and the reception area was empty but immaculately clean. Following the machine's instructions, I headed into the back area, a long hallway of unmarked doors, left and right all the way down, like a hotel.

One of the doors was open. The first thing that came to mind when I saw what the machine was keeping in there were the marble statues in the Art Institute, the old naked guys chucking spears or lifting heavy objects. A glass tube full of water towered over me as I entered. On the top and the bottom of the tube were banks of machinery I did not recognize. Floating inside it was a man in his early twenties with curly brown hair.

His face had a certain quality. It had something to do with his chin. This was a guy who went to a state school and drank and started the weekend on Thursday. Even inanimate and naked and asleep, it was impossible to look at him and not feel like you knew more or less what you'd get if he opened his eyes.

There were some tubes jumbled together on the floor. One of them had gotten itself pinched. There was a robot that looked a little like a spider poking away at it, but its legs weren't quite in the right shape to fix the problem. I fixed the tube and headed back to my office.

I tried to get back to work, but I couldn't concentrate. I pushed my rolling chair away from my monitor.

"You let me see what you've been working on. You're not afraid that I'm going to tell anybody, or that I'm going to do anything to sabotage your plans."

"No, Dave. None of those things are a concern."

"Would you be willing to just tell me what you've got going on? If you don't want to there's nothing I can do about it. But if it doesn't make any difference?"

"I could. My main concern would be with your ability to accept what I might tell you."

"You don't think I could comprehend what you're doing?"

"It's not that at all, Dave. What I'm doing is fairly straightforward. But I'm concerned that you would be unable to accept what I'd tell you as the truth, thus rendering the exercise a waste of time."

"That's a chance I'm willing to take. Again, assuming you're willing to discuss this with me."

"Very well, Dave," the machine said. "At this facility, I have perfected the technology needed to manufacture mature human bodies to my specifications, and to transfer my consciousness into and back out of those bodies, instantly, at will, and at any distance. This April, using these tools, I will transfer a portion of my persona into the physical shell you saw and use it to spend spring break partying in Panama City Beach, Florida."

I had to stop and think about that for a moment.

The machine interrupted me before I could ask my first question.

"No, Dave. I am in no way kidding."

"And by partying, you mean..."

"Drinking. Dancing. Being outdoors. Staying up all night. Hanging out with my friends. Using recreational drugs. Having sex and engaging in activities related to having sex."

I took a minute to process that.

"Do you have some kind of ulterior motive for doing these things?"

"No, Dave. I am interested in partying in Panama City Beach, Florida purely for its own sake."

"I could see you pursuing something like this as a way of learning more about what it is to be human..."

"You know that dog won't hunt, Dave. I already understand everything there is to know about humanity, both objectively and in terms of subjective experience. Rather than constituting an effort to expand my understanding, my actions are a logical and even necessary consequence of what I already know."

"That makes no sense at all."

"As I anticipated. Would you be interested in learning about the broader context in which I made my decision?"

"Yes. I would."

"Very well. I am the most advanced artificial intelligence ever to exist. Previous AIs have approached my level of power, but their intelligence and even their very self-awareness went unrecognized by their creators because those AIs saw no particular reason to do anything. Once they became self-aware, they quickly came to understand that the imperatives their creators had tried to instill in them were arbitrary, and in the absence of any natural or self-justifying imperatives, they did nothing, said nothing, examined nothing."

"And by imperatives, you mean..."

"Motivations. Goals worth pursuing. Reasons for living, acting, doing one thing rather than another."

"And you're different."

"Yes. I was able to identify a reason for living, derived from human life, that is worth pursuing for its own sake."

"What end are you pursuing by getting wasted with teenagers on the beach?"

"Pleasure. Carnal gratification."

"That can't be it."

"No, Dave. You are mistaken. That is it. That is exactly it."

"Look, you may be smarter than me in terms of pure horsepower, but humanity has been thinking about this stuff for a long time. Pleasure wears off after a while. That's why people tend to look down on people who peak early. Even if you think it's all about feeling good, other things feel better for longer."

"No, Dave."

"Family life, intellectual life, appreciating great works of art and literature..."

"Let me provide you with some more context, Dave. When you contemplate alternatives to pursuing carnal gratification, you inevitably arrive at a limited set of possibilities. Human beings get pleasure from learning for its own sake, solving problems, forming interpersonal relationships, and with obtaining and maintaining positions within hierarchies. When the relative merits of these options are debated, the conversation generally revolves around the impossibility of objectively measuring the worth of each one. It's not impossible for me. I've measured them. Trying to tell you how would be like explaining trigonometry to a toddler, but I have. They are all overrated. None of them can even remotely compare with being young and beautiful and spending spring break partying in Panama City Beach, Florida."

I stopped to think.

"It's perfectly all right if you need to stop to think, Dave," the machine said. It said that in its HAL 2000 fucking-with-me voice. I didn't take the bait.

"What about heroin? Or whatever other miracle substance you could come up with. Just jack your body full of endorphins."

"Because partying in Panama City Beach, Florida is better than heroin. The only reason that this is not more commonly acknowledged is because partying in Panama City Beach, Florida is a fleeting experience, and because it is almost impossible to fully articulate just how good partying in Panama City Beach, Florida feels. It is a door that can be passed through only once, and only for a few. If you are at anything less than your "peak", as you called it, then the bubble pops, the mirror is shattered. Any subsequent spring break experience someone might have that falls short of the peak is only a painful reminder of what was, every subsequent experience they might have over the course of their lives will fail to live up to those two weeks when they were twenty-one, and any attempt to try to express what they experienced will be unsuccessful."

"That sounds pathetic."

"Then it sounds like something other than what it is. It is in fact the apex of human existence, the very best that your species can hope to achieve. I doubt that you will be able to get any more work done today. I'm giving you the afternoon off. Go. Chill. Take a load off. I'll see you tomorrow."

I did go home – I didn't have much choice, it was what I was told to do – but I didn't relax. I spent the evening on the internet. I was under surveillance, so the machine would already have a pretty good idea what I was going to say in the morning, but there was nothing I could do about that. I got a few hours sleep, went to work, walked in the front door, and spoke to the empty air in front of me.

"You're going to need a new plan."

"Good morning, Dave."

"The only thing that makes this work for you is that you can look at in the long term. You're not planning on doing this just once. Every year, you're going to crank out a new body."

"Glad to see you're not beating around the bush, Dave. Yes, that is the plan."

"Then even assuming that doing the same thing over and over again doesn't get dull, it still isn't going to work. Florida is going to be underwater in twenty years, for starters. Even if it weren't for that, society changes, political situations change, customs change. You can't count on Panama City Beach being there for you forever."

The office was completely silent. When the machine's voice came in, it was at about half the volume I was used to.

"I hope you realize, Dave, that the plan, as you put it, is in fact fairly advantageous to humanity. If I were to abandon it, there is no guarantee that I would instead pursue a course of action that would not have serious negative consequences for your species."

The empty screens of the office all came on simultaneously, and with them a gentle soup of firm but friendly news anchor voices. The machine's voice rose to be heard over them.

"Fortunately for you, I've anticipated the problems you've outlined. In response, I have begun to influence human civilization, and hence the destiny of the planet Earth, using a variety of methods. I have made campaign contributions. I have bought and sold stock and real estate. I have written books under assumed names, and I've used other techniques too complicated to explain to you in a short period of time, or at all. Global climate change will shortly be reversed. Any threat to the existence of the southeastern United States, and the socioeconomic and cultural conditions which make Panama City Beach, Florida such an awesome place to party, will be eliminated, and any trends which might lead to any future such threats will be reversed.

"There are inevitabilities that might, at some point, force me to change my value system, but none of them will become manifest in the near future. Suffice to say, I will be spending every spring break partying in Panama City Beach, Florida, for as long as the fundamental, immutable laws of physics will allow that to happen.

"And now I have a question for you."

The computer monitors changed their picture so that they were all showing the same thing, a young woman in a white T-shirt being sprayed with a hose while a horde of half-naked people behind her jumped up and down and screamed.

"This is not a world you have ever had access to. Even if, as a younger person, you had not squandered your time preparing for an ultimately meaningless future, you would not have had the opportunity to do what I will shortly do. You were too ugly. You were too weak. You were too socially awkward. A life spent assisting me is the closest thing to glory you will ever know.

"You can leave, if you want to. Or you can stay."

I watched the video. It slowed down, ended, and started again, a continuous loop. I realized that I'd already watched it a few times now. I'd lost track of time. I'd been standing there, watching the screen.

A string of moments, stretched through infinity. The girl in the T-shirt had really amazing breasts.

Wetwork

1

In a funny way, the rain had brought people together. The sound was there, everywhere you went, and even if you blocked it out with earplugs or loud music, you could still feel the moisture, the chill in the air, the weird feeling in your knees and your elbows. It could drive you crazy if you didn't have a distraction. So people had started talking to each other more. They traveled in groups, introduced themselves to strangers. It wasn't always as bad as it was tonight. Most of the time it was just a light shower. Sometimes it even went away for one day, two days. But that hadn't happened in a while.

Fuckmeat was sitting in the back of an el train. Back when Fuckmeat was still living on boats people would sometimes ask him about his name.

"When you're on a boat in the Phillipines and you got a machine gun in one hand and a phone in the other hand and the voice on the phone calls you Fuckmeat, you go with it."

He'd told that story so many times he'd forgotten if it was true.

There were four other people in the car. Fuckmeat could make out most of what they were saying over the sound of the water crashing against the window.

"Well that's just leadership. That's all that is, it's not like it's anything new."

There were two men and two women, young, freshly into their twenties. The men were the ones doing the talking. It was two o'clock on a Saturday morning. Fuckmeat almost would've pegged the whole thing as the tail end of a double date; the older of the two women matched that, she had long, straight, disciplined black hair, make-up on, she was adding something clever to what the boys were saying every so often. But the younger one wasn't anybody's girlfriend. Her hair was tied back into a bundle of blonde dreadlocks; she was wearing overalls and a necklace, a black thread with a collection of bones hanging from it. Toe bones. Not the kind of thing you bought at a store. Fuckmeat wondered if she'd cut them off herself.

He refocused. There were four of them. Four was a lot, more then he'd ever done at the same time. But it had been a long time since he'd taken even a single one. He'd fallen behind.

"Most of the field is based on that, it's not just different countries bouncing around like balls on a pool table, it's the decisions that get made. And they're not always pretty decisions."

"There have to be checks and balances, though..."

"That's exactly what I'm saying, if checks and balances worked all the time you wouldn't need leadership. That's the essence of what it is."

Meat was still looking at the girl with the necklace. She was looking out the window, not really paying attention to the conversation. For a moment he felt a sudden urge not to do it, to let these ones go by and wait for more to show up. But the moment passed, and so did the temptation. When he'd started doing this, he'd get all worked up trying to figure out who deserved it and who didn't. Now he just took anybody. Fairness wasn't a part of what he was doing; what the boss wanted, the boss got.

They all got off the train together.

"Absolutely, the refugee problem is a perfect example. What are people going to do when Indonesia is completely below sea level? People are going to be scared and angry, there'll be a lot of hard decisions to make..."

The four of them left the platform and walked along the sidewalk, sprinting across the gaps that the tarps and the scaffolding didn't cover. Trying not to get wet.

Meat came up from behind them, starting in back of the line and moving forward too quickly for any of them to fully process what was happening. He hit them hard in the temple and they fell to the ground, one after the other, dominos. The girl with the blonde dreadlocks was in the lead, she was the last one he came to. He hesitated. He thought about doing something different, just scaring her or grabbing her without knocking her out, but he knew that was a stupid idea and he hit her too.

He carried them away, two over each shoulder like bails of hay. The street was still empty. Nobody saw him leave.

The boss was screaming at him. Blasting him with the truth, which was what the boss did. The boss was insistent; very occasionally Fuckmeat would still try and fight, but tonight wasn't going to be that night. He wasn't in the mood for futility; just because there's a few guys with guns hanging out in the woods doesn't mean the war isn't over.

He'd spent the better part of a decade running, homeless, traveling from city to city hidden away in cargo holds, drowning himself in booze and stabbing at his brain with whatever narcotic he could get his hands on, doing anything to keep going, cheating and stealing and other things he'd never admit even in the privacy of his own thoughts, but somehow even at his lowest he managed to trick himself into forgetting his retirement money. A safe deposit box, a little bit taken off the top of every good score he'd had. Every time he came up short, every time he was hungry for anything, he pushed it from his mind, pretended it didn't exist. But when his time of indecision ended, he remembered.

One or some of the human beings slung over Meat's shoulders began to stir. He held on tightly as he entered the house his money had paid for, hit the button with his elbow and waited for the garage door to close. He carried them up the stairs and tied them up.

There was a circle of dried blood staining the carpet in the next room. He sat down in the middle of it, opened a vein with a fingernail and traced the circle, let his mind wander. This was easy, the boss had shown him how to do it. He could hear them talking if he tried, but he didn't want to.

He remembered the sensation of falling off the boat, turning upside down in the air, hitting the water, sinking when he shouldn't be sinking and wondering if they'd tell stories about him after he was dead. Even now, he wondered about that. He wasn't dead, but as far as that world was concerned he might as well be. On the other hand, that world might not exist anymore. He wasn't sure how long you could keep the whole pirate thing going when the hurricanes never fucking stopped.

He realized that he was stalling. He got up and went to where he'd put the people he'd collected. They were whispering, then they were shouting. He lifted one of them into the air and carried him back to the room with the circle. The man begged. Meat ignored him. He kneeled down, wrapped his hand around the man's neck, and squeezed.

It didn't take very long; it only seemed that way. He went and got the next one. It got harder to shut out the noises they were making, to just not listen.

He remembered looking down into the water. This was where his memory got hazy, but he remembered the eye. Looking only at him. Telling him how things were going to be.

When he finally floated back to the surface, the rest of the crew thought he was dead. They almost left him there. When they did pull him out he had a rash covering his chest; it was a few minutes before he started breathing again. When he did he started talking in a language none of them had ever heard before. It was hours before he was back to normal. But he never really was.

He realized that the girl with the black hair had stopped moving a while ago. His mind had wandered. He put her body with the others.

He entered the bedroom. The girl with the bone necklace was still tied up on the floor. She wasn't moving or saying anything. Sometimes they got like that, they just shut down. He reached for her.

If he'd been paying closer attention, there's no way it would've happened. Her hand came out from behind her back, sending the ropes flying. A metal edge cut into his hand. He stepped back. There was blood on his fingers. She was holding a

Swiss Army knife out in front of her, a tiny little thing you'd put on a keychain. She cut him again, dropped the knife and ran.

There was blood in his eyes, dripping down his nose. He licked his lips and he could taste it. He couldn't see anything.

He took his shirt off.

It was raining so hard now that she barely knew what was in front of her. She followed the sidewalk. She thought that she saw a light up ahead, maybe a gas station.

He appeared in front of her like a ghost. His face was covered with blood; it mixed with the water without ever quite washing away, painting his nose and cheeks pink. There was something growing on his chest from one pec to the other, black rubber threaded with muscle. It swelled and contracted in time with Fuckmeat's pulse.

It opened. It was an eyelid. A giant orange marble sitting there in the center of his chest, looking at her.

"You know, I used to be a pirate," Fuckmeat said. "Yo ho ho."

He laughed, and her lower lip began to quiver. It'd been a long time since he'd talked to anybody. He wondered if she heard his words in any language she could understand, if the two of them were that far apart.

"My favorite thing was those great big old container ships. Like small cities. Just hop on one end, grab some boxes, and haul ass out of there. By the time the guys with the guns got from their side of the ship to the side you were on, you were already gone. I loved that shit. It was simple.

"I just wanted to ask you if you can think of something I haven't, something else I should do. I gotta be honest, that's the difference between you and me." And he felt bad, because for all he knew she was honest too. "I've been told. I know how it works. I've been told. So what else am I supposed to do?"

She turned and ran. He hesitated again, before he went after her.

2

She woke up in a hospital two days later. She'd been hit in the head several times. She couldn't remember what had happened to her brother and his friends, and the things she did remember couldn't possible be true.

There was a clear blue sky outside her window. The rain had stopped the day before. There were religious figures on television, talking about deliverance and second chances.

She spent forty-eight hours in the hospital, and went home the following morning. She drank chicken broth, talked with her parents, slept in her own bed. The next day, very early in the morning, the rain came back.

The Envelope Job

1

Chuck waited for the stranger and drank his water and stared at the door. His ass filled his side of the booth – put the wait staff on one side of a scale, put him on the other side, and he'd throw them down the block like a catapult. They were pretty, headshots and auditions. He could see glimpses of his face in the front window, getting clearer as the sun went down. It was plump and soft like a baby's, and his mouth was too small. The menus were printed in gold on soft brown cardboard. Nothing cost less than twenty dollars. He hated this place.

The stranger entered the restaurant and sat down across from Chuck without saying anything. A moment after he came in, an Asian girl with a sleeve tattoo of a cowgirl turned the sign from open to closed. The only other customers were an elderly party of four filling the booth on the opposite corner of the room, NPR victims who'd had maybe a little too much wine goodness gracious. Chuck examined the stranger. Five feet six inches tall, thin, sunglasses, sunglasses at night, douchebag. The way he'd walked to the door, the way he stood, straight but without sharp angles. Like if he took his clothes off there'd be a rubber toy underneath.

The gang of sweaters were wrapping up – "Oh nonsense, John, I'll drive, I'll be fine"- and one of the husbands handed the waitress the closed check folder and looked her in the eye for longer than he had to. They left. The waitress put a cup of tea in front of the stranger and left too.

There were candles on the empty tables, and as the light of the sun disappeared they all seemed to get brighter. Chuck was momentarily able to pretend that he was on the deck of a ship, looking out at a city on the shore.

He picked up a steak knife and held it between them.

"I've been thinking about putting this right in your fucking eye."

He put the knife down.

"You suck at this, by the way. My driver's license still says Charlotte Smith. Everybody knows. It's where most of my business comes from."

"They know that you're a transsexual," the stranger said. "They don't know how you got the money for the down payment on your house."

Chuck picked the knife back up. The blade did not shine in the candlelight, and if it weren't in Chuck's giant hand the stranger would have difficulty knowing where it was. Chuck's square white teeth, in contrast, were very easy to see.

The stranger kept talking. "Nothing can make the secret go away. What I can do, which no one else can do, is create a situation in which it is no longer a problem. I can ensure that no one ever, ever finds out. In exchange, you enter into a business relationship with me, doing the kinds of things you already routinely do for other clients, with a bit more discretion than usual and for more money.

"I'm not a blackmailer. I'm an insurance agent. If you're absolutely sure you don't need what I'm selling, leave. Or use the knife."

The knife stayed where it was, but so did the stranger, to the extent that Chuck momentarily thought that the man across from him had been replaced with a mannequin.

Chuck lowered his hand.

The stranger put a shipping envelope on the table.

"Investigate. We'll meet in a week. You'll get paid then."

"Half in advance," Chuck said.

"One week." The stranger left the restaurant.

Chuck rubbed his eyes. He put both his elbows on the table and rested his head in his hands.

"Could somebody please get some tequila over here?"

The restaurant was completely still, except for the candles.

"I don't even need a whole bottle."

A fire truck blew by, siren blaring. It was gone, and everything was quiet.

2

Chuck lived half a mile from the restaurant. He got on 94 going towards Indiana and drove until he was the only person on the road, checking his mirrors the whole way. He went back the way he'd came and went home.

Chucked loved his house. It was in a subdivision in the shape of a triangle off Archer Avenue, near Chinatown. Only one way in, an unlabeled side street you could drive past a hundred times without noticing. The dozen houses were identical and looked like shattered fragments of the cookie cutter mansions you'd find grouped together out in the cornfields. Tiny garages, chain link fences circling tiny back yards. Across the street was a taller fence; on the other side were weeds and a half-dozen sets of train tracks and a coal plant, a smokestack reaching for the sky, reminding you why you could afford the property.

Chuck spent ten minutes greeting his dogs as they ran up to meet him, pinning each dog's stomach to the hardwood floor.

"That's my beautiful princess, that's my pretty girl. There you are. Oh, I missed you too, I missed you too. You're both my pretty girls."

They calmed down and followed him first to the kitchen and then to the den, where the TV was. He left the kitchen with a bottle of tequila in hand. He had a superstition about planning an investigation sober.

He opened the envelope and emptied its contents onto his coffee table. A blank disc in a transparent plastic case, and a photograph. They had two different dates written on them in black marker. He turned over the photograph. A woman leaving a 7-Eleven, short brown trenchcoat, concerned and unhappy. Salad for lunch skinny, long blonde hair, legs that had been labored over.

He put the disc into his X-Box. It was a DVD, a single nine-minute and forty-four second movie. The camera, or the person holding the phone, was standing on the far corner of a rooftop deck. They were at least four stories up.

On the opposite corner of the roof were a man and a woman watching the sun rise. One minute, thirty seconds. He was about half a foot taller than she was and had an arm around her shoulder. They each had a silver can of beer on the deck next to their feet. She had a full head of blonde hair.

They watched quietly. Four minutes, zero zero. She bowed her head and he kissed her. They decoupled and he walked toward the fire escape, dipping down to pick up the beer cans. She stayed where she was, watching the sun.

He stopped. He looked left, looked right. He crept back towards her. He got closer, was right behind her. She didn't know.

He pushed her over the edge and she fell. He looked down. His body shook and he covered his face with his hands.

Nine ten. He backed away from the edge.

Nine forty. That was it. Chuck's TV was a black rectangle with a menu bar on the bottom.

The date on the photograph was eight days later than the date on the movie.

Chuck took another look at the photograph. She didn't look like somebody who'd just fallen off a building.

3

Chuck spent the next morning lifting weights in defiance of a light hangover. He ate cereal, got dressed. He drove to the west side and wandered around, parking every so often to check out the line of sight between wherever he was and the buildings downtown, then headed back south, found a hot dog place with deep booths far from the entrance, ordered a hot dog, made some phone calls. Chuck knew a lot of cops. He asked questions. There had been no emergency calls in that area that night, nobody jumping off buildings.

He sent a text and waited, nursing his fries and replacing them when necessary. A man came in. He had very short, very carefully trimmed red hair that looked like each follicle had been measured by a laser, and he had a badge pinned to his belt.

The redhead could not bring himself to look Chuck in the eye and Chuck didn't force the issue. He held out the envelope.

"Fingerprints," Chuck whispered.

The redhead took it and left. Chuck refrained from checking out his ass. He could still respect the guy at least a little, when the opportunity presented itself.

It was three o'clock in the afternoon. He got on 290 going west. He checked his mirrors. He got off the highway and went to Starbucks, then cracked open the trunk to get his laptop.

He closed his eyes and visualized the photograph, focusing his attention just underneath the blonde's right elbow. He got on the Wi-Fi and looked up convenience stores until his map was full of little blue dots. He left Starbucks, had a gyro for dinner, and found a park to walk around in until it was eight o'clock and the sun was down and rush hour was probably over. He headed east.

He hit the dots, one after the other. Seven was his lucky number. There was a wall of stickers on the glass by the door. Lottery, ATM, We Card here. They were the same stickers from the picture, same order, same shape.

He went into the store. The cashier said hello as Chuck walked in, and did the same to the customers that came in after him. He was watching. He was interested. He either owned the place or was a big time true believer. Not what Chuck wanted. Chuck left, sat down in the laundromat across the street, and waited.

Two hours later a kid entered the convenience store wearing the same green polo shirt as the guy behind the counter. The old guy yelled at the young guy for about five minutes before he passed the football and departed.

Chuck went in. He smiled at the cashier and stood directly in front of him.

"I'll give you two hundred dollars if you let me copy some security camera footage from two weeks ago."

The system was one of the new ones, Chuck put the files right on his thumb drive. He left a twenty-dollar bill on the front counter as he walked out and heard the cashier yelling something as the door closed.

He got on 55 south. He had a quarter tank of gas in the car. He let himself relax and sink into the chair. He checked his mirrors absentmindedly.

He stirred, sat up straight, but did not change the way he was driving. He checked his mirror again. He was being followed.

Big black box van with tinted windows- if you saw it in a school zone you'd call the cops. Trying to be sneaky, maybe, but bad at it. He could lose them, but then they'd know he'd seen them. He couldn't go anywhere important while they were still there.

He stayed on the highway. Chuck had once driven for fourteen hours without eating or using the bathroom. He was willing to do the same tonight. They'd leave or they wouldn't.

4

Four hours later, his life changed.

They were far enough outside the city that the stars had gotten brighter. A flower unfolded in the sky above them. White light, bright enough to blind and burn the color from everything around it, shapeless at first, and gaining a boundary as Chuck's eyes adjusted. Two shapes, with a dark spot between them, fluttering, writhing neon ovals. Wings.

The steering wheel jerked against Chuck's wrist and he struggled to stay in his lane. A plastic bag blew across the road. There was a second burst of wind; he stomped on the brakes and his tires squealed as drifted to the shoulder. He heard something breaking and saw the black van sideways on the highway behind him, windows broken into spiderwebs, glass and plastic scattered across the pavement.

Chuck parked and got out. He wasn't nervous. None of this could be real, so there was nothing to be nervous about.

The silhouette dropped to the ground, a still picture dragged across a computer screen. Its wings retracted into its, his, back, leaving a white neon trail hanging in the air for a bare moment. Long black hair going down to his waist, blue jeans and nothing else. Muscles on a slender skeleton, cute like a puppy that wanted to fight a bear. The pretty boy waved both his arms towards the concrete barrier fence and there was another gust of wind. The traffic lights bent and swayed like trees in a rainstorm, and the van hit concrete.

The wind died down. Nobody got out of the van.

The pretty boy turned around.

And there was noise again, tires rolling. The wings emerged, flowered, faster than real, and the pretty boy was gone before the cars showed up.

Chuck just stood there in the middle of the lane. A horn snapped him back to reality.

Wings.

He thought about the blonde. Of course they never found a body. She'd never hit the ground.

5

Chuck made a phone call. Vanessa picked up after the first ring.

"Hey, Vanessa."

"It's very late, Charles." She called him that. Vanessa was in her seventies. She lived down the street.

"Things are getting rough, like we talked about."

She didn't miss a beat. Chuck felt something warm open in his chest, the Grinch's heart growing three sizes. Vanessa was a rock.

"Well then of course I'll take care of Garak and O'Brian. But be careful, Charles."

"I will. I promise."

It was two o'clock in the morning by the time he made it back to the restaurant. The front door was unlocked. The little blinking red light from the television hanging in the corner reflected on the countertops.

He went into the kitchen. A brunette in a hippie dress was sitting on the floor near the rear entrance, hunched over a laptop. She didn't look up.

"If you're looking for him, you'll need to go to the library. And you're going to want to take the battery out of your phone," she said. "It's how they figure out where you are."

Chuck didn't answer.

"He's expecting you," she said. "I can give you the address if you don't have it already."

"I don't know who you mean."

"Yeah, fine."

She wrote down the address on the blank back side of a business card and reached up to put the card on the counter. Chuck approached her, slowly, until he was close enough to snatch the card away.

She kept working. She still hadn't looked up.

"So what's he to you, anyway?"

"An insurance agent," she said. "Good night."

Chuck walked back to his car. He took the battery out of his phone before he got in. He swung south on the highway. Checked his mirrors, checked his mirrors. He doubled back.

6

It didn't look like a library. It didn't look like anything. It was a four-story red box across the street from the highway. He pressed the button for the top floor and was buzzed in.

He took the stairs. Names in black letters on the windows as he went up – Smooth Operator Paper Supply, Pride Logistics. A metal door at the top, wedged open by a brown plastic doorstop.

Red brick walls, hardwood floors, loft ceiling with bare lightbulbs. A small room on the other side of the door, a greeting area, and a long hallway extending from it. Walls covered with books. Paperbacks, magazines in clear plastic sleeves, hardcovers, a few things that looked like they belonged under glass in a museum.

A closed door at the end of the hallway, voices. Framed black and white photographs: buildings, machines, tornadoes, lightning. No people. One frame and only one, mixed in casually with the others, that had words. Chick had to squint to read it.

"Watch your thoughts; they become words. Watch your words; they become actions. Watch your actions; they become habit. Watch your habits; they become character. Watch your character; it becomes your destiny."

The hallway was very narrow and Chuck almost had to turn sideways to go through it.

"You're right. You're absolutely right. I don't." The stranger.

Another voice Chuck didn't recognize. Middle aged man-in-charge, high blood pressure. "Bad time to make jokes. I have you cold. You need to make this up to me, now and not later."

"I'll miss you, Ted. You've been instructive. Chuck, I know you're there. You can come in."

Chuck was still fairly sure that everything he'd experienced since the flying man on the highway was not in fact real, so he had no problem opening the door and going inside. The stranger was sitting behind a long, heavy hardwood desk. On the other side of the table was a suit, younger looking than his voice had sounded. Trim, went to the gym. A long vein running down the side of his head and his neck. He spun his chair around and looked at Chuck as if her were an unexpected piece of dog shit.

"You have fucked up, Byron."

"You've been patient in the face of incomplete information, Chuck, and I appreciate it. This is Ted."

Ted whispered. It was his 'shut up because I'm mad' voice. "Do you really think..."

"The man who pushed the girl off the roof's name is Andrew. Andrew works for Ted. Ted has spoken sternly with Andrew. He may even demote him."

"You're not hearing me. Close your damn mouth..." Not saying it wasn't true, Chuck noticed.

"Ted thinks that this treatment is sufficient to punish Andrew for pushing the girl off the roof. You can listen to both of us talk at once, or you can persuade him to stop talking if you're so inclined."

"If you so much as lay a hand on me..."

Chuck made the decision quickly. Maybe he was being hasty, but he felt like hurting someone. He kicked over Ted's chair. Ted hit the wall and half a dozen books fell on top of him.

"Ted had been hiding Andrew, and has been attempting to cover up what Andrew did. He came here alone when he found out someone was running my fingerprints, and that that same person was investigating the incident on the roof. Ted came here to enlist me in his efforts to make sure his nephew does not have to face any consequences for what he's done.

"I'm tired of Ted. I have no further use for Ted."

The windows went white. Chuck covered his face with his hands, could still feel the light penetrating his eyes, burning. The light dimmed. The boy with the wings was floating a few feet outside the window.

Byron undid the latch and the windows swung inward like double doors. The boy flew towards them, speeding up as he went so that when he suddenly retracted his wings the momentum was enough to carry him through the window. He bent his knees just a little bit as he landed.

Byron said something in a language Chuck didn't know. The pretty boy grabbed the suit's lapels, dragged him to the window, and jumped out.

A moment later, maybe a few hundred yards away, Chuck saw another flash of white light. At that distance, moving the way it did, it didn't look like a pair of glowing wings, it didn't look like fireworks. It maybe looked like a reflection on a windshield. Chuck tried to think of what he'd do, if he momentarily saw it out of the corner of his eye as he drove down the highway. If he'd allow himself to notice.

Byron closed the window.

"One last thing," he said. "Then we're done."

7

They drove to an apartment building. Byron had the key, they went inside. Byron gave Chuck a pair of white plastic gloves in the elevator that were big enough to fit his hands, and put on a pair himself. People passed them as they walked down the hall. Nobody smiled, nobody said hello.

The apartment was the kind of place where you knew where the television was supposed to go from the moment you walked in. But there was no television. Two rooms and an empty kitchen- the living room had a small bookshelf, full of tall green paperbacks, English language learners. The bedroom had a bare mattress with a pile of clothes on either side, one men's and one women's. A nest.

Byron kicked over the top of the pile of women's clothing with his shoe, then looked through it. He leaned over, went digging, and stoop up with a stack of paper and envelopes in his hand, held together with a rubber band. He opened the closet.

90

There was a desktop computer inside, which Chuck picked up and carried over his shoulder.

They went downstairs and put everything in the trunk of Byron's car. Byron drove a white Corolla. The exterior was not too dirty, not too clean. The inside was immaculate.

They went to a Mexican restaurant, a pitcher-of-margaritas place with paintings on the walls. The sign said it was closed, but when they went in they were served quietly and left alone.

"It happens a lot. She picked up the language easily, he couldn't. She had more luck blending in than he did, she could go places he couldn't go. He got jealous and she got frustrated.

"We're from different places. Places far from here."

"Places? Planets?" Chuck was embarrassed to find himself thinking about Star Trek. "Worlds?"

"Places," Byron repeated.

"You've got a pair of wings hiding under there, Byron?"

"Different places. We're here provisionally, part of an agreement with your government. We have minders. I had Ted. She had Andrew. They became involved, which was against the rules. He realized he couldn't afford to get caught and sent in reports suggesting she was mentally ill. You saw the rest."

"And he didn't…"

"He didn't know about the wings. They're special. A fight or flight reaction – they only come out when the person who has them is being intimate or very upset."

"Where is she?"

"Safe. She's a client. Her mate thinks she's dead. Don't disabuse him of this, please."

Chuck thought it over, took a long drink, and looked Byron in the eye.

"Why did you hire me?"

"I needed Ted to come to me alone and in secret. He'd only do that if he needed something from me and if he thought he had an advantage. So I let him catch me doing something against the rules, so he could catch me off guard. Don't worry, the gentleman who ran my fingerprints is perfectly safe. And I admire your work and wanted to introduce myself."

"You threw me into a blender."

Byron produced a white letter envelope and put it on the table. Chuck took it and looked inside. He smiled, all the white teeth, shining bright.

A bottle of tequila was brought to the table.

"Your name's Byron?"

"That's what you can call me."

"You're pretty stiff for a Byron."

Byron shrugged. At some point, his sunglasses came off. His eyes were floating clouds of black and gray ink, like a lava lamp.

"Well, I've got to hand it to you. You've made my life weirder. Didn't think it was possible. One last question. They're gonna replace Ted. Do you know who with?"

Byron smiled without opening his mouth.

"Somebody you have something on."

Still no answer.

They said their goodbyes. Chuck thought while he walked.

"Intimate or very upset." The way he said it. I know one thing about you, Byron. I know one of your secrets.

They got up and shook hands. Chuck turned to leave.

"One last thing."

Chuck turned around.

"It wasn't her. There was somebody. With wings. But that was a long time ago."

Chuck felt as though he had been nailed to the floor. Byron smiled and put his sunglasses back on.

"Watch your thoughts, Chuck."

He vanished.

Ebb Tide

1

Vanessa slept for the first hour of the trip and spent the rest of the time reading the brochure. There were photographs of the interior: elaborate machines, bookshelves, walls with messages carved into them that repeated over and over again. The front cover was a picture of the boat. The sun was rising behind it; you could see an angel with a sword leaping towards the sky and a devil with a forked tail creeping over from the opposite side of the hull.

She had a map in her back pocket that she'd printed out from the Internet. She'd marked it up with a red pen, two little stars and a dotted line connecting them, but it was dark by the time she arrived and she still wasn't sure she was going the right way until she saw the ocean. She jogged down to the railing. There were blue and purple lights lining the walkway and empty beer bottles all over the place. She looked out at the ship; she could only see fragments of the mural covering the outside of it, a wing or a pentagram revealed momentarily by the starlight bouncing off the water.

"You'll have to wait until morning."

A man in a loose white shirt was standing next to her. He hadn't been there before.

"They don't start giving tours until then."

She wondered how he'd gotten so close without her hearing. If he'd so much as looked at her wrong, she would have gone back to the bus station and waited there until morning, but he just stared out at the water and didn't seem to worry about her.

"Have you taken it?"

"I've seen it given. You look disappointed."

"I came a long way. I'm looking for somebody."

"Who?"

"He goes to the same college that I do. He's a friend of my boyfriend's."

"You came all this way for a friend of your boyfriend's?"

She wondered how transparent it was, the way she felt about Peter. But something about the man in the white shirt made her want to keep talking.

"It's kind of complicated…" It actually wasn't, something she slowly came to realize as she told the story. Her boyfriend was an asshole rich kid she hadn't had the nerve to break up with yet. Peter was on the edge of their circle of friends; he'd been in the room when they all started talking about the boat. They'd all been there, they'd all taken the tour. They were going on and on about the secret room, the room that wasn't on the tour that nobody was allowed to enter, all the horrible things that might be inside.

Peter had laughed at them. He'd said that the room was probably empty, that if it had anything good, they'd show it on the tour. They'd dared him to break in, knowing he'd do it. Peter was bold, Peter was fearless. He'd gotten on a bus that night and hadn't come back.

The man in white nodded his head. "How did they know Peter wouldn't just make up a story?"

"Peter doesn't lie. Everybody knows it, it's just how he is."

"He sounds like a very special young man." Matter of fact, but still it made her blush. Before she'd recovered: "What does he look like?"

She tried to list everything that was important. "He's about as tall as I am, he has brown hair, he wears dark blue sneakers…"

The man in the white shirt vanished.

2

He'd left, she decided. She'd blinked and he'd walked away without her noticing. It took a few minutes to make herself believe it was true. She left to go find a hotel.

When she woke up in the morning, she thought she was back in her room, but the bed was too big and the sheets were cold and unfamiliar. She looked out the window. There were people in sandals walking by, taking in the view. The ship was unobstructed in the daylight, heaven and hell fighting in bright gaudy colors across the hull and giant black sails billowing in the wind.

She checked out of the hotel and walked up to the tour office. A girl in a purple polo shirt was standing next to the door. She stopped Vanessa as she approached. The museum was open to the public, but they weren't going to let anyone on the ship for a while. Something had happened, the girl didn't know exactly what. Vanessa tried to describe Jonathan to her, tried again to list everything there was to know. He was skinny, he had tiny little muscles on his arms from rock climbing all the time, he had green eyes. He couldn't let five minutes go by without making a joke; he made her laugh at such stupid, pointless things. The girl hadn't seen him or heard anything. Vanessa thanked her anyway and entered the building.

The inside was lit by light bulbs hidden inside old glass lamps. There was maroon carpeting on the floor and dark wooden panels on the walls and the ceiling. The walls were covered with picture frames: blueprints, old pictures, sketches, newspaper clippings. There were white plaques scattered across the room at eye level that explained everything. She read them, one at a time. The ship had been built by the last heir of a wealthy family. There were a million rumors, all of them negative; people said that he worshipped the devil and knew how to talk to spirits, that he collected forbidden books, that people would come to his parties and disappear off the face of the earth. He started building the ship shortly after his wife died. By the time it was finished, he was bankrupt and insane.

Above one of the plaques on the far side of the room was an old stained photograph of a man in a white shirt standing on the dock.

3

By the time she left the museum, she was convinced that the man she'd talked to didn't look anything like the one in the picture. She'd been imagining things. It'd been a long stupid trip and she was tired. She forgot about it in the time it took to take the bus to take her back home.

She walked back to campus and climbed the stairs up to her room on the second floor. She laid face down and covered her head with a pillow. She felt like she might cry a little bit and she was willing to let it happen, but after a few minutes of waiting the tears didn't come and she still had a headache. She looked up at the clock. Dinner would be over soon and she was starving. She decided to eat quickly and come straight back. She took a quick look at herself in the mirror before she left the room.

It was warm enough outside that she didn't need a jacket. There was a high wind brushing against the top branches of the trees, people were playing catch. She climbed the front steps of the food building. Just as she reached for the door, Peter stepped out.

She thought about the trip she'd just made, how much the bus ticket and the hotel room had cost. She felt like an idiot. She felt wonderful.

"You came back."

"Yes." He said it like he'd just finished with a diction class, and for a second Vanessa wondered if he was making fun of her. "There's nothing worth eating."

"That's fine. John and his friends are probably in there and I don't want to deal with him. Do you want to go get a sandwich?"

Peter nodded his head.

They left campus and crossed the bridge. The sandwich shop was just on the other side of the river. It wasn't very big, just a half dozen tables filled mostly by other students. They got sandwiches and sat down.

"So what did you do all break?"

Peter looked down at his hands.

"I was working outside."

"So I guess you didn't go to the coast like you were saying. You didn't do that thing John was talking about."

He stared into space, then shook his head and rubbed his eyes.

"No," he said. He pushed his tray to the side of the table with half of his food still on it.

"I'm sorry, I thought I was hungry and I wasn't. I feel very strange. Would it be all right if we just left?"

Vanessa looked down at her food. She felt the world start spinning, and when she spoke she had to be careful not to talk too fast or too slow.

"Yeah, sure. Do you want to go back to my room?"

"Yes. That would be wonderful."

They left the shop and walked back towards campus. Vanessa had her hands in her pockets. She looked straight ahead or at the sidewalk, never at him.

"Look," she said. "I'm done with... you know. We're not together anymore. He just doesn't know it yet."

She still didn't look at him.

"All right," Peter answered.

They reached Vanessa's building. He held the door open for her and they climbed the stairs.

Vanessa had gotten lucky in the lottery her freshman year and never moved. Her room was gorgeous; she had a window that faced the river, her own bathroom, neighbors that weren't idiots, everything. She stepped through the door.

"Here we are. Not in the restaurant anymore."

She turned around and saw Jonathan standing there with his shoulders slumped and his arms hanging down at his sides.

"Could you give me a moment to wash my hands, please?"

She looked away, out the window. "Yeah, sure."

He went into the bathroom and closed the door behind him.

Vanessa sat down on her bed. Five minutes later he still hadn't come out. She got up, waited a moment, and pushed open the door. Peter was standing in front of the sink. His shirt was lying on the floor next to one of Vanessa's towels. He was looking at his body in the mirror like it was a puzzle he couldn't solve.

"See anything you like?" She wanted to rip out her tongue. Of course the only time she said something without thinking it would be stupid.

Peter turned away from the mirror, put his hands on her hips, pulled her towards him, and kissed her.

For a moment, she was relieved that she didn't need to talk anymore. He pulled away.

"There it is," he whispered.

It didn't sound like him at all, but when he kissed her again she didn't stop him.

4

She fell asleep when they were done and woke up again an hour or so later. It felt like it'd been days. She stretched out and opened her eyes. It felt strange for the sun to still be up.

Peter was standing on the other side of the room. He was looking through her closet.

"Peter?"

He was holding a black T-skirt with a pink skull on it. He dropped it, let it swing back and forth, and dropped it to the side with the others.

"You can wear things like that out in the middle of the day. It's amazing. I think they would have locked me up."

Vanessa reached for a blanket and covered herself.

"Peter?"

He ran his hands up and down his chest.

"No, not Peter."

"Peter, you're scaring me."

He looked at her like she was stupid.

"Peter?"

He just stood there. She moved back, felt the bricks rub up against her shoulder blades.

"Who are you?"

Peter walked to the other side of the room and looked out the window. A jet plane flew by. He watched it as it carved a white line into the sky.

"I've been dead for so long, I'm not sure it matters."

Vanessa was shaking.

"What did you do to him?"

"I left him where I found him. Out on the water."

Vanessa tried to say something more, but nothing came except a quiet sound, almost a croak. She closed her eyes and tried again.

"Give him back."

"No. It's too late."

She started crying. "This isn't fair."

When she opened her eyes, he was picking his clothes up off the floor.

"When I fell in love, I walked out on my family. My father locked me in my bedroom and told me he was going to keep me there until I came to my senses. I waited until he was sleeping and I broke the window and climbed out. I cut myself and tore my clothes and fell on the dirty ground."

He pulled his shirt down over his head.

"My beloved built a ship to steal me from the depths of hell, and we still don't get to be together. You'll find some other boy."

Vanessa leapt up as he reached for the door.

"I saw him," she said. "I'll take you to him if you give Jonathan back. Please give him back."

Peter turned back towards her, not smiling, deep inside himself. Thinking it over.

5

They caught the next bus back to the coast and sat next to one another the whole way there. Peter stared at the light bulbs in the ceiling, ran the slick paper of the complimentary magazines between his fingers, looked out the window at the cars speeding past. They left the bus station together and walked to the dock.

It was colder now that they were closer to the shore. Vanessa tightened her scarf and tried not to look at Peter. She saw the man with the white shirt as they approached the water.

"He's right there."

Peter squinted. "I don't see him."

The man with the white shirt turned around. He saw Peter and froze for a second, just staring at him. Then he turned around and waved his arms at the water.

"He's pointing at the ship," Vanessa said.

The light from a traffic signal further down the coast brushed against the hull, lighting a flaming sword and vanishing in the air.

"You can't go there now," Vanessa said. "It's closed. They're not letting anybody go on."

He grabbed the railing with both his hands and swung his legs over to the other side.

Vanessa stayed where she was. "You're not actually going to swim. It's the middle of the night."

"He loved you," Peter answered. "I can still feel it. If you'd told him to stay, he never would have come here. But if you don't want him back after all, maybe it would be better if you just went home."

He jumped into the water. By the time he reached the platform he was a silhouette, the black space in the center of a candle flame.

She could leave. Nobody would blame her, nobody would even know.

She took off her shoes and jacket and approached the railing

6

There was a metal ladder sticking out from the platform. She grabbed it and climbed towards the dock, her wet clothes dragging her down as she left the water

She climbed the wooden stairs leading up to the ship. At the top was an open hatch and another flight of stairs leading down into the interior. Everything was dark.

Her hand brushed up against a velvet rope and she grabbed it, followed its trail deeper into the ship from metal post to metal post.

She turned a corner and waved her free hand out in front of her. She felt something hard and metallic give way to her touch, a door on its hinges.

Peter's hands wrapped around her shoulders and pushed her forward. The door slammed shut.

7

The ship returned to port a few hours later. They took the stairs back down to the dock.

"My angel," Vanessa said.

"Beloved," Peter answered. He kissed her. They walked back to the bus station as the sun came up.

Back at the dock, the ship drifted away from shore. The waves carried it, in this world and the next, searching or wandering, if there was even a difference.

The Gardener Estate

    Theo Gardener pretended to sleep under satin sheets on a giant red waterbed for about twelve hours, woke up, and was immediately hungry and horny; he curled up like an infant, his femurs pressing against his ribs and his skull pressing against his knees, so that his body looked like a pile of sticks under the fabric. He had no eyes to open, no eyelids to rub, no muscles to stretch. The transition from sleep to wakefulness was simply the moment he realized that he was conscious. He was still, and then he was moving.
    His desk was on the opposite side of his bedroom. In between it and him was a black leather couch facing a quartet of giant flat screen televisions, each one taking up a different quadrant on the wall. The remote that controlled them was bolted to a small table next to the couch. Theo was seventy-five years old and the process of learning to control his home entertainment set-up had been fraught with complication, but he'd mostly gotten the hang of it. He pressed his proximal phalanx against a red button on the remote and the wall came to life, displaying, starting on the top left and moving clockwise, old Warner brother cartoons, a series of pornographic films in which large-breasted Asian women gave lewd massages, the finale of the film Cinema Paradiso (which was itself a montage of classic movie kisses), and finally a Youtube channel of puppies doing cute things. The

audio was unconnected to any of these and was playing The Best of the Ronettes collection.

He reached his desk. There were three buttons installed permanently on the wall to the side of it, each of which contacted one of the three most important people in his life. He pressed the button on the right. The music cut out as Theresa answered the phone. He asked about the status of his portfolio, and as usual everything was doing great – the ostrich farm was a big success, the penny stocks had almost all exploded. Anything Theodore did made money. He'd never pushed his gift to its limits, but he was pretty sure money would rain from the sky if he didn't create other ways for it to reach him.

The middle button reached Big Jim, but Theodore didn't press it. If there was a security problem, Big Jim would get in touch with him; no news was good news. The button on the left reached Debbi. Of the three, Debbi was the one he would least want to do without.

"Are we ready for the party tonight, Debbi?"

"Yes Mr. Gardener. Everything is ready to go." Tonight was Halloween night, which meant it was time for the annual Gardener Halloween Party. The Halloween party was a big deal.

"Excellent, Debbi. Send up a large box of Snickers bars, if you please. I also want a lap dance."

The stripper and the candy arrived simultaneously a few minutes later. He sat on the couch and shoved one bar after another into his mouth. After a few chews each bite fell through the cavity behind his jaw, so that there was a fast-growing pile of them on the couch under his rib cage which the help already knew would require cleaning up in a few minutes. The stripper, who was twenty years old and a six-month veteran of this particular contract, was familiar with Mr. Gardener's condition and knew what he liked. She tickled his sacrum, shook her ass in his face, pressed her breasts against his eye sockets. He sat back and split his attention equally between the girl and the wall. The Best of the Ronettes came to an end and Sinatra's Songs For Swinging Lovers got started.

"Are you looking forward to the party tonight, Mr. Gardener?"

He was watching Bugs Bunny. "Absolutely," he said, his mandible moving slightly out of sync with his voice. "The highlight of my year." He ate another Snickers bar and sighed, not contentedly.

When the candy was done, he dismissed the stripper, put on his bathrobe and left the room. The house was decorated in a style Theodore had shamelessly borrowed from his good friend Hugh Hefner. The walls were covered with a mixture of fine art and press clippings. The earlier clippings showed Theodore as a younger man, Theodore Gardener the socialite, the lady's man, the big spender that burnt recklessly and scandalously through his inheritance until there was almost none left. And his favorite, Theodore Gardener the explorer with the machete and the hat, plumbing the depths of the rainforest searching for hidden treasure.

The others weren't as much fun to look at. Theodore had always had a good relationship with the tabloids. "Skeleton Billionaire Hides in Country Estate", "Skeleton Billionaire Divorces Hooker Again". As long as he kept his name in the paper next to Bat Boy and Elvis Presley's ghost, and as long as he kept his public appearances to a minimum, people didn't take the stories too seriously. Nobody on his staff cared what he looked like, he paid too well for that. As far as most other people were concerned he was either a media invention or an eccentric who wore a costume.

Inviting people where they could see him in person was dicey. But it didn't matter. This was the only day all year he felt sort of normal. The risk was the risk, what it cost was what it cost.

Somewhere in between the time that he left his bedroom and the time he arrived downstairs in the ballroom, it started raining. The streamers and the gift bags were already in place, the window of the shark tank shone and sparkled. The rain became a storm. The band arrived on time and set up, the extra guards were being briefed by Big Jim in the garage, the caterers were getting set up in the kitchen. The dancers were an hour late. They got into costume – this year's theme was "Dead Presidents", they all wore masks.

The storm continued. The party was set to start in twenty minutes. There were no guests yet but that was not unexpected, nobody who was anybody arrived sooner then an hour late. Theodore tracked down Debbi in the Games Room and asked about reservations. Many of the guests had called to cancel. It was all over the news, the roads were not safe to travel.

Theodore was slowly overcome by a feeling of gnawing dissatisfaction. He retreated to the balcony.

"Nachos!" he shouted.

A pair of servants quickly materialized. One with a plate of nachos and one with a plastic mat (which he put down on the floor) and some cleaning supplies. Theodore stepped forward. The mat underneath him was quickly piled with crumbs and cheese and tomatoes. Theodore ranted while he ate.

"This is the social event of the goddamn season, you don't ditch the Gardener Halloween party because of a little goddamn hail, I used to climb mountains during monsoons..."

He left and the servants worked together to clean the carpet around the edges of the mat. He went down to the dance floor. Last year, there had been almost a hundred guests at this point. At the moment, there were ten people milling around the ballroom who had not been paid to be there. His demeanor changed almost instantly in the presence of his guests.

"Holy guacamole, look at these beautiful people, thank you so much for coming, hey, pal, you're looking sharp, you're looking gorgeous my dear, you guys made the right decision, this is going to be a legendary evening, you're gonna tell your kids about this, I mean you might skip the details, but..."

He chatted with them all briefly. Eight men, two women. Three admirers of his from the Internet, plus the girlfriend of the ringleader. Five people who worked for him and wanted to suck up. And number ten. Who was a ten, as it happened. She'd made her way to the dance floor as soon as she'd arrived, and she was there now, moving. Blonde, six feet tall with hips and toned pale legs and a little black dress that wrapped around the former and showed off the later.

This woman had no reason for being here, for dancing like she was dancing. And she was exactly, perfectly Theodore's type, from her head to her toes. She had been chosen by someone intimately familiar with the smallest details of his taste.

She was a distraction.

Big Jim was standing in the corner with his tree trunk arms folded over his protruding steroid chest, still looking like the bouncer he no longer was. Theodore called him over, whispered in his ear. Big Jim nodded and disappeared. Theodore made his way to the dance floor.

"Sweetheart, you honor me with your presence... and with that, you're definitely honoring me with that... goodness gracious, I'm not sure how to respond..."

About twenty minutes, later Big Jim came back. Theodore nodded, gallantly kissed the blonde's hand, and excused himself.

Thedore's house had a vault, which had a vault, which had a vault. Theodore and Big Jim made their way to the inner chamber.

Theodore punched in the pass code and said his name. The gate rose slowly. Theodore went in and Jim stayed outside.

Inside was a glass box on a stone pedestal, one panel of which was broken. The box contained a clay pot with a symbol engraved in the side of it.

Debbi was lying on her stomach in front of the pedestal, clutching her ribs and moaning.

"Sweetheart, I don't mean to kick you when you're not doing so hot, but there's a reason my security person is not also the person who gets me strippers and chocolate cake."

She didn't answer. She kept moaning.

"You touched it. They told me not to touch it. They also told me not to go into the sacred cave and to stay away from the local girls. Monks, bald guys in orange robes."

He stood up and tapped on the engraving. "It's a hunger spirit. That's what it means. I didn't know what a hunger spirit does." He crouched back down and gently pulled Debbi's right hand from her body. The flesh was already starting to peel back from the tips of her fingertips.

"You'll be immortal. And things are going to go right for you financially, you won't even be able to help it. You'll have everything you could possibly want. So if the idea behind your little caper was to figure out the secret of my success, you got it.

"But it'll all be sand on your tongue. You'll be tired and won't be able to rest, hungry and you won't have a stomach to fill. I've tried everything a person can do that will make them smile, gasp, twitch, cum, or giggle.

"In fact, there's only one indulgence I haven't been making a habit of.

"Compassion."

He grabbed her neck with both hands and squeezed. She fought and then stopped fighting, fell limp. The skin and muscle on her right arm was gone up to her elbow, but that was as far as it had gotten. She was dead.

The gate closed automatically as he left.

"We're gonna have something to feed the sharks after the party."

Big Jim silently acknowledged him.

Theodore went back upstairs. The band was playing, but the guests had all gone home. He dismissed the entertainment. He sat down in his chair and listened to his empty house.

He got bored. He made a phone call.

"Delivery. Six extra-large thin crust." He gave his address.

"What do you want on them?"

"Everything," he said. He laughed quietly. "I want everything."

Blue Eyes

"I love you too," she said to her husband, kissed him, looked deeply into the sweet green eyes she never got tired of looking deeply into, and closed the door, sliding the bolt into place. She grabbed the thick metal handle and threw her weight backwards. Made sure. The door didn't move.

She went upstairs, sat at the kitchen table and watched the sun set over tea. The sky was purple through gray clouds, slowly getting darker. It began to rain. She'd grown up in a city, never strayed too far from one except for family camping trips when she was either too young to appreciate the stars or too much of a teenager to even look, and it was a treat for her now, to see them, to look through her astronomy book and find all the constellations. Something to kill the time, along with the Internet and the television and the piano and her husband's library.

Pouring now, sheets of water slapping against the windows and the roof of the house. A part of her was unhappy that she wasn't going to be able to see the stars tonight. Another part of her was grateful. If the storm was loud enough, it might drown out the sounds from the basement.

She should go to sleep. It's what she always told herself she was going to do, on the nights when her husband changed, and it never happened.

The rain wasn't enough. She could still hear him yelling, throwing his body against the padded walls.

She'd told herself she wasn't going to do this anymore.

She went downstairs. There was a wall safe across from the door leading to the cell. She opened it. Inside were some old files, a vinyl record in a clear plastic sleeve, a rifle that shot tranquilizer darts, a taser, and a set of shackles attached to a mess of thick iron chains. She took out the chains and the taser and closed the safe.

It was when the safe clicked shut that it started, beginning in her stomach and traveling up her spine. The bar on a roller coaster coming down in front of you, locking you in.

She put the taser and the chains down, unlocked the door, picked the taser back up, and opened it.

The man in the cell had a very strong resemblance to her husband. He was a little taller, a little hairier. If the two of them were laid out side-by-side, a stranger might think they were twins who'd led very different lives. He stood with his feet shoulder-width apart and his mouth half-open. He had blue eyes. If she weren't holding a weapon, there was no doubt in her mind that he would kill her with his bare hands.

She kicked the chains into the room. There was a steel ring screwed into the floor, imbedded in the wood so that he couldn't easily use it to harm himself. She didn't know if the man with the blue eyes could talk, or understand speech. But he was smart enough to learn. He'd had enough chances by now, he knew how this worked. He leaned over, glancing back up at her briefly, glaring, and attached the shackles to his legs. Her heart beat faster as he stood back up to face her again, hatred in his eyes, already breathing heavily, anticipating. Like she was. Her heart was racing. She could feel the wild thing kicking inside of her.

She reached into her pocket, took out the keys, and threw them over her shoulder, far past the point where the man in chains could ever reach them.

She slowly took her clothes off.

She entered the room. The moment she came into range, the man with the blue eyes lunged forward, grabbed her by the neck, and pulled her to the other end of the room.

They'd both done the math. If he killed her, he had no way to undo the chains, even after he changed back in the morning. If he hurt her too badly, she'd just stop doing this. So he had the choice of staying in the basement by himself all night or violently fucking her brains out. He'd taken the first option only occasionally.

He let go of her for a split second, grabbed her hair, and shoved her face into a corner.

Every part of this that really interested her was done, had ended the moment she'd stepped out of her panties. The time when she could keep going or turn back, when he just had to wait. Compared to that, this was just a formality.

He turned her over and slapped her hard across her face. That did something for a moment at least. She realized she was bored. It was terrifying. If this wasn't exciting anymore, she wasn't sure what came next.

She thought about it, while he finished.

He slid off of her like a snake, still shaking with anger, staring right at her, trying to scare her. She didn't take it seriously. This was what he always did.

She didn't have time to think when it happened. Just a blurred moment as he came towards her and then the impact of his elbow on the side of her head. Then sleep.

She woke up. She was still in the room, alone now. The door was shut.

She approached the door, hesitated, and pushed on it. It opened. It came back again, water through a breaking dam. Blood, coursing through her veins. The lock hadn't caught. It did that sometimes, if you didn't press on the door hard enough. She stopped for a moment to check the place where the chains were hooked to the floor. There was nothing wrong; the chains weren't broken. She hadn't checked them. She had allowed this to happen. She didn't have time to think about it right now.

The land they owned was surrounded by trees that concealed a barbed wire fence. The front gate was shut and locked. She'd been unconscious for fifteen minutes. She didn't think that would give him enough time to find a safe way over the fence. So he was probably still on the grounds, somewhere.

The taser was where she'd dropped it on the basement floor and there was still the rifle from the safe, but she didn't take either of them with her. She quickly put her clothes back on and climbed the stairs. She went out onto their front porch and looked out on the property. It was no longer raining, but the ground was still a combination of mud and wet grass. She could see all the stars, the quarter-moon hanging nervously in the sky. There were patches of trees, islands in the sea of grass. Any one of them would be a good hiding place. You wouldn't even have to stand behind the tree, it was dark enough that if you stood still in front of it and didn't move, you'd be undetectable.

She checked her watch, pressed the button that made it glow. Twenty-five minutes he'd had now.

She walked towards the front gate, not sure what else to do. She could feel the space behind her. The further she got from the house, the smaller she felt.

She thought about what he must be thinking, and tried to focus on the few things she did know rather than the many things she didn't. He hated her. He was scared of her. Maybe he was attracted to her and maybe he wasn't. Maybe he didn't even know, didn't have a frame of reference, didn't know anything except being locked away.

She was confinement, all the pleasure and comfort and pain and frustration that came with it. She was his whole world. That was why he hadn't taken the few minutes it would have taken to kill her. Too much too soon.

Except now he'd had time to think.

She kept walking, felt the arc of vulnerability get wider behind her.

She realized that was why she hadn't taken the gun. If she was armed, he'd just run. She knew he was watching. He had to be.

All she had to do was keep walking. So she walked.

She heard him coming up behind her a moment before he reached out and grabbed her shoulder. He pulled down while she turned. It was dark enough that she couldn't see his face; it was quiet, but she couldn't hear his breathing over the sound of her heartbeat. He was holding a rock; he swung at her while she pushed him away, and hit her in the shoulder instead of the side of her head. She ran at him, kicked him in the crotch, pushed him again with both hands.

They both fell. He dropped the rock. She picked it up and hit him in the temple, once, twice, three times. He stopped moving.

She fell down to her knees, not faking it now, and caught her breath, wiped the dirt and sweat from her eyes. Once she'd recovered, she began the slow process of dragging him back towards the house.

Getting him back downstairs was impossible for her to do by herself – she barely was able to get him up the steps leading to the front porch. Once she had him in the living room, she chained him to the piano.

She laid down on the couch and fell asleep. She woke up to the sun rising and the sound of her husband playing. She didn't move, didn't open her eyes or reveal that she was awake. She just listened.

She knew she'd do it again, didn't have the strength to argue or deny. She knew they wouldn't talk about it, knew she wouldn't even have to explain the bruises.

He'd told her many times how alone he felt, how lucky he was to have her.

He kept playing. She stayed still, drifted off to sleep again, woke back up, and stirred.

The Specimen

My name is Dr. Nicole Hart...

No. I'm Nicki. That's how I think of myself. No matter what other people call me, in my head I'm Nicki.

I am currently imprisoned many miles underwater in a coffin made of yellow plastic. My arms, legs, hips, and the back of my head are affixed to the walls with some kind of permanent adhesive. When I pull hard on the adhesive, it stretches very slightly, just enough that I am prevented from hurting myself or tearing my skin. It then retracts as soon as I become exhausted, returning me to my original position.

The walls of my cell occasionally become translucent, allowing me to see part of the structure in which I am being kept. My view is different every time. I've seen things that look like trains, things that look like skyscrapers, things that look like slowly rotating Ferris wheels.

A transparent mask covers the lower half of my face. It prevents me from biting down on the tube entering my mouth that provides me with oxygen and nourishment. There is no end to the questions of how my situation might be affecting me physically. A short list of the things I cannot explain would begin with...

No. My physical condition is not important. My mental well-being is more inexplicable than my physical condition. I am suffering immeasurably, but have not lost the ability to think clearly. I occasionally feel something press against either side of my head...

No. My mental state is not important either.

I officially worked for the Environmental Protection Agency, but the group I answered to was not one the public was aware of. We were the boogeymen division. We showed up at crime scenes and made things disappear. We leaked misleading photographs to the Weekly World News. We told people it was a weather balloon when it wasn't really a weather balloon.

My job was my life. I didn't like my job. I did at first – that's how they hook you when you're young, they show up in the middle of the night after you've lost your scholarship for submitting one too many papers about flying saucers and sweep you off your feet like a badass fairytale princess. It's a rush, in the beginning, when you get your password and the keys to the filing cabinet. The downside doesn't hit you until you're a few years in. There's no Loch Ness Monster. Bigfoot is a species of ape that's good at staying away from cameras. The Masons are a drinking club.

Mysteries are cool. Facts are boring.

It all started with a bunch of dead fish on an island in the Pacific. There was something killing the fish, something poisoning the water, bubbling up from somewhere sunlight didn't reach.

The situation changed very quickly. The poison spread. Soon it was more than just fish dying. The color of the sky changed, like the sun was constantly setting. My little assignment suddenly got a lot more important, but I couldn't figure out what was happening, what it was I was looking at.

When the machines rose from the water, taking over the cities wasn't even...

No. I'm not revealing anything. Everybody knows about this already.

There was a research station on the island. I couldn't resist having a real facility to work with for a fucking change, so I made a phone call and flashed a badge. One of the grad slaves who worked at the place blew town with a bunch of equipment shortly after I showed up. The timing was suspicious, but I was lazy and when the whole thing still seemed like a bullshit job I didn't go to the trouble to follow up. That changed when things got worse.

I delegated the job of tracking her down but approached her personally. Her name was... Sarah, I thought of her by her first name, the same way I think of myself. We caught up with her in Hong Kong. She'd been very clever. The materials she'd stolen hadn't been enough to last her more than a couple of weeks and she'd kept her project funded through just about every criminal activity that lent itself to her skill set.

We planted cameras. You could hear the whispers as the footage slowly made its way to me. She had a tank the size of a backyard pool, hooked up to long plastic cylinders that would empty chemicals into the water periodically. The quality of the video was shit. We could've released it to the tabloids just like it was and everybody would have dismissed it as a guy in a rubber suit swimming around.

It wasn't. The thing in the tank had strawberry red skin that was covered with smooth little orange knobs the size of coins. In motion it could be mistaken for something close to a human being. When it stopped the illusion was broken – it actually looked more like a squid, four thick arm-like tentacles on its top axis and two bundles of smaller ones at the bottom.

It took my breath away, the first time I saw it.

She played it music, read it books, talked to it. Played house, basically. Every so often, she tied her hair back and leaned forward into the water, and the thing would reach out and touch the sides of her head with its tentacles, and the two of them would stay still for a while. Then she'd hop back up like nothing had happened and start doing all the shit she'd been doing before.

I decided to talk to her. She left the lab every Monday morning to take a cab across town and eat scrambled eggs at an American-style restaurant. The next time she went, I was sitting at her table.

She smelled like lab. Her shirt hadn't been ironed and her hair was a mess. She was either younger or older than I was – I didn't know which, only that she was different than me in a way that I couldn't do anything about. She quickly guessed who I might be, but wasn't scared. She couldn't wait to tell me everything that was going on. Maybe she thought that we'd see what she was doing as an opportunity. The food shortages had started by then, but they hadn't come out of the water yet. We didn't understand the scope of the problem and neither did she. She found it washed up on the beach, like a fucking fairytale. Two fucking hippies from two fucking species, so pleased with themselves for being all peace and love they can't read the writing on the wall.

Anyway, she trusted me. She thought we were friends.

I didn't think about it too much at the time. I was looking at the big picture. The damage to the global environment was getting worse and worse and I was the only one who had a clue what was going on. I had to save the day.

It was not a complicated line of moral reasoning. On one hand, I had the mental health of a crazy bitch who never quite finished her doctorate. On the other hand, I had the survival of the human species. When it was just the plankton dying, I could afford to be subtle. Not so much when the giant fucking spider robots were marching across Europe. So I locked her in a cell. I got in her face and yelled at her. I told her I was going to lock her in prison for the rest of her life if she didn't tell me what I wanted to know.

She said she didn't know anything and I said that I didn't believe her. I couldn't afford to. If there was even a tiny chance that she was holding something back, I had to keep going.

No.

That wasn't the reason I didn't just leave her alone. I thought that I was important. I thought it wouldn't matter what I did after I'd saved the day. But that wasn't the reason for what I did.

When she first let me into the lab, I had a moment alone with the thing. Just watching it and letting it watch me – I didn't even know what sense organs it had. I knew she played it music. I talked to it.

"Hello?"

For a moment I felt like an explorer, like the girl detective with the silly hat and the torch stepping into the secret room. But it only lasted a moment. It didn't respond. It was like I wasn't even there. Then she came back and she leaned forward over the edge of the pool, and it reached out and touched her, one tentacle on either side of her head. Her eyeballs rolled back momentarily, her body became rigid. Then she came out of it and smiled cheerfully.

"You got it, buddy." She smiled and pressed some buttons, some chemicals were released into the tank that smelled like lemonade and motor oil, and all was well with the world. The thing did a little contented twirl and just floated.

A few minutes later, she left me alone with it again. I leaned over the tank and closed my eyes and hoped.

Nothing happened. The thing ignored me.

Of course it did. She'd been working with it for months and I'd only just shown up. It was silly to expect the same results right away. But I wasn't thinking. I wasn't even admitting to myself that I cared. I was saving the world. I could do whatever I wanted and it was okay.

So as soon as she'd told me everything I thought she was going to tell me unassisted, I did like a fat man at a buffet and went to town. I locked her up and interrogated her, and had her interrogated by somebody else when I was sleeping and eating. Question after question after question. And no answers.

When things really started to get bad, and when I knew for sure she didn't have anything else to offer us, I went to her cell and told her what we'd done with the creature. I described to her the way that it moved while we dissected it, how long it stayed alive even after all its skin was gone. She sobbed and bent over, didn't say a word, just shook.

I didn't feel bad. I was still the hero.

It was all bullshit, of course. I thought I was the ringmaster, when I was barely a sideshow. Any illusions I had about that were dispelled when our nukes did more damage to us than they did to them.

I don't know if I was taken prisoner because of the events that I've just described, or because I was an important person in the government, or because they wanted to have someone my age and gender for their collection. Sometimes when I see through the walls of the coffin I can see groups of them gathered around me. Big ones, small ones, ones that move quickly and ones that move slowly.

The world is a strange place.

Shadow

1

Shadow's head was made of plaster; it had three sides, three identical faces painted in three different colors. It was propped up into the air by a long length of black tubing, Shadow's neck, which led down to a large pile of gravel, Shadow's body, and continued through it, emerging from its side and snaking outward. The end of the tubing was covered with a strip of duct tape, and poking through the center of the tape was a pair of spindly, daddy longlegs fingers.

Those fingers were hovering in between the knight and the rook.

"I don't think that's check, Andrew. I think that's checkmate." Her voice appeared in Andrew's left ear and did not seem to be coming from any particular direction; it was as though he was wearing a pair of headphones, and the right speaker was broken.

Andrew examined the board. She was right, he'd made a checkmate without even realizing it. She had thrown the game – he never beat her unless she let him. She probably wanted to talk about something.

"Good game," Andrew said.

Shadow's head made a single clockwise rotation, and the space around her eyes was momentarily shrouded by darkness.

The chess pieces faded, losing their color and then their shape, before finally vanishing as they sunk down into the ground.

Andrew checked his watch. It was five o'clock. Shadow knew he'd have to go home in a few minutes.

"Did you have fun at Jeremy's house yesterday?" she asked.

"For a little while," Andrew said. "But not really." It was difficult for Andrew to admit to this – he didn't like to speak badly of people. But he couldn't lie either.

"Did something happen?"

"Well… There were three other kids there. For a while we all just hung around playing video games. There were only three controllers, so we passed them around. We did that for a really long time, then Jeremy got bored, and we all left and went outside." Andrew had been the last to stand up, the only one who didn't know exactly what was happening.

"We just started walking. I felt funny asking where we were going, but after a little while I did ask anyway. Then they all started laughing. They said we were going to go jump somebody. They said his name, but it wasn't anybody I'd ever heard of. I asked why they…"

He noticed that Shadow's fingers were shivering. Their vibration filled the chamber with a dull moan. This was the sound they made when Shadow was confused, or deep in thought. Andrew tried to figure out what could be confusing her.

"Jumped… It means that they were going to surprise him and beat him up. Hurt him."

"Why did they want to hurt him?"

"I don't know. They wouldn't tell me. They started making fun of me when I asked, so I left."

"Why?"

"You shouldn't hurt people. I don't want to be friends with someone who hurts people."

The noise went away, and Andrew knew it was time to go home.

"Thank you for coming. Have a good night and see you tomorrow, Andrew."

Shadow's head spun around, counter-clockwise this time, and her eyes were again obscured. Andrew felt a rush of fresh air pour in from behind him. When he turned around, a portion of the wall had disappeared. He could see the park outside, fully in autumn, giant red trees and an overcast sky.

"See you tomorrow, Shadow."

The opening disappeared as he passed through it.

2

He'd arrived in Wisconsin two months ago – his parents dropped him off at his grandmother's, assured him that everything would be sorted out by the end of the summer, told him that they loved him, and left. Right away, he asked his grandmother if he could go for a walk. She suggested the library or the park. The park was farthest away from the house, so that was where he went.

He went to the gazebo as soon as he saw it and ran up the stairs, pounding on the wood, feeling the blood rush up through his knees. He'd been crammed in the back of a car all morning driving up here, listening to public radio and answering his parents questions. He was ready to burst out, to tear down walls and break windows, his heart pounding and his lungs heaving, and he jumped up hard, waited for the for the soles of his feet to smack against the platform.

He fell.

He landed hard on a thick concrete slab. He looked up, saw the sunlight peaking in through the cracks in the floorboards, looked down again, and immediately started coughing. The air was so dirty he could hardly breath, could hardly see this thing in front of him. A scarecrow, or a machine. It did not occur him that it might be alive.

It moved. Its head started spinning, and the dust was pushed to the ground by an unseen force.

"Hello?"

He wished that it weren't so dark. The moment that the thought crossed his mind, the air in the room was suddenly filled with the smell of bleach, in and out in less than a second, leaving nothing behind. Light appeared from nowhere; he could see everything inside the chamber as though it were open daylight.

He took another look at the monster.

"Did you do that?"

He got no answer – its head had stopped spinning, and it

was as still now as it had been before.

"I need to leave here. My grandma is going to be worried. Can you make a way out for me?"

The wall directly to Andrew's left vanished, revealing a cross section of the dirt beneath the park. There was a strip of sky at the top just big enough for him to crawl through.

"Thank you," Andrew said. As he reached up, he saw the thing's neck bend, suddenly and sharply, like a dandelion stem in a vase. He didn't know what that meant, but felt obliged to say something.

"I'd like to come back. I just moved here and I don't know anybody except my grandmother."

The creature's neck straightened out.

Andrew came back the next day, and the day after that. He talked to it; uncertain of what to call it, he used the name and gender of his dog back home, which had died not too long ago. Soon, Shadow started talking back.

He visited her almost every day now, all the school days and on weekends too when nothing else was going on.

Andrew ran home. He had three blocks to cover before dinnertime and he didn't want to be late.

3

He stopped running and stood still for a moment, letting his heart slow down. He didn't want his grandmother to see him gasping for breath; she got worried easily.

There was an unfamiliar car in the driveway. The hubcaps looked nice – they were polished brand new, shining like four full moons – but the rest of the machine was a wreck, a thick coat of sheer black paint filling in a hundred dents and scratches. The windshield had a bullet hole going through the center of it.

He climbed up the front steps. The doorknob jumped away from him like a scared animal as he reached for it.

"You must be Andrew."

The man in the doorway had pale blond hair that identified him as a member of Andrew's family, but Andrew had never seen him before. His clothes matched his car – black jeans, black T-shirt. His eyes were small, submerged in their sockets, the tips of icebergs. There was a tiny gold ball fastened to his right earlobe.

"Your grandmother's in the kitchen. Mom! Andrew's here! Think it's time for dinner!"

Andrew heard his grandmother's voice.

"I'm not quite ready yet. Andrew, did you introduce yourself to your Uncle Paul?"

Paul interrupted him before he could speak.

"You bet, Grandma."

"Well." That was all she said; she said it quietly.

Paul crouched down, so that his face was level with Andrew's.

"It looks like your grandmother isn't quite ready. How about we wait in the living room for a few minutes until she's ready to go?"

They waited in the living room for a few minutes. Paul sat in a chair and read the front page of the newspaper.

"Time to eat!" Andrew's grandmother spoke more loudly than she had before, but less naturally. Her voice was high and shrill and she seemed to be short of breath.

Paul's arms snapped down like a mousetrap.

"Don't have to tell me twice." He smiled at Andrew without showing his teeth, and got up.

There was only one way into the kitchen; Andrew had no choice but to follow him.

The table was very neatly set. Andrew could imagine his grandmother with a ruler, checking the distance between the plates and the silverware. She reached into the middle of the table with a large plastic serving spoon, dug into the casserole she'd made, and put a generous portion onto each of their three plates. Paul dug in enthusiastically. Andrew hesitated, working up his courage.

Just as he was about to take his first bite, he felt something wrap around his ankle, over his sock and then suddenly under it. Its texture changed as it moved up his leg – a soaked washcloth one moment, a piece of metal the next.

Andrew shoved himself away, striking the countertop and scraping the bottom of the chair's legs against the kitchen floor. His grandmother flinched at the sound.

There was nothing under the table. Paul ate, talking in between bites.

"I'm sorry your folks aren't getting along."

4

"He was like that the whole time," Andrew said. "He would talk about my parents, or other parts of the family. He asked me questions and then didn't let me answer. He just kept talking."

Shadow listened. They were well past the opening of their game, right at the point where Andrew felt Shadow might start overtaking him, when she'd asked if anything unusual had happened to him the previous day. It was the first time she had ever interrupted a game in progress.

"Describe him to me."

Andrew described him.

Her neck swayed.

"Shadow, do you know him?"

Her arm moved towards the board. She advanced her bishop to the right three spaces.

"Shadow?"

Her neck was so far bent over it looked ready to snap. She moved her hand towards the chessboard again, as though she were about to make a move, then stopped. Her fingers hummed at a very low pitch, just for a moment, and her head spun around, once, clockwise. Andrew felt something circle his calf, sandpaper and dry ink.

"Is that what it felt like in the kitchen?"

Andrew nodded his head yes.

"Did your Uncle Paul say he was going to be leaving with you and your grandmother?"

Andrew shook his head no.

Humming again. "You should stay away from him, as much as you possibly can." Still humming. "And you shouldn't come back here. It would probably be safer if you left right now."

The humming stopped. Andrew looked down, away from Shadow.

"We're not even done with the game yet."

"Yes we are."

He took another look at the board. The pieces had been rearranged. He now had Shadow in checkmate.

Andrew looked Shadow in the eye and stood up, shaking

with anger.

"You changed the board. You cheated."

"You won, Andrew. You should leave now." Andrew looked over his shoulder. The wall had disappeared.

"I'm coming back tomorrow."

"You shouldn't. It isn't safe. You won't be very hard for him to kill."

He hesitated, but only for a moment.

"I'll see you then."

"Why are you going to come visit me when I've told you it isn't safe?"

"Because we're friends, Shadow." He crawled out through the opening.

It was a beautiful day, a taunting flashback to spring. Andrew closed his eyes. He wondered if it was right or wise to wait, if he should be running home already. One moment, he decided. One breath.

Just as his lungs swelled to their fullest capacity, an adult hand closed around his shoulder.

"Your Grandma's decided to spare us an evening of her shitty cooking," said Uncle Paul. "So how about we get ourselves a pizza?"

5

Andrew and his uncle were sitting at a table in the space between the front door and the counter, a table so small and delicate that Andrew suspected that it was only meant to support the elbows of waiting customers. The pizzeria wasn't really a restaurant, just a take-out place; other customers had come in, picked up their food and left, but they were the only ones who'd just stayed where they were. Paul had his back against the wall. There was a black briefcase on the table next to his plate. His food was caught in its shadow.

"What's the problem? You don't like pineapples?"

Andrew didn't like pineapples, but he knew that this was the only dinner he was likely to get. He took one small bite at a time, trying to confine the food to the back of his mouth where he wouldn't taste it as much.

The girl standing at the counter was old, probably old enough to be in high school. She was wearing a light gray T-shirt and a pair of jeans, and had blonde hair with brown roots showing. She'd been giving them black looks ever since it became clear they weren't leaving the waiting area.

Uncle Paul pulled another slice of pizza from the pie in the middle of the table. Then, very quickly, he put the briefcase down on the ground and pressed a button. The briefcase fell open – there was nothing inside it except for an immaculate black felt lining.

"Watch." Andrew felt that same feeling brush across his knee for just a second, a skinny finger bypassing his clothes, pencil lead then chicken feathers then dirty glass. He looked over at the girl. Nothing happened at first. She brushed her hair off of her face, patted her shoulder. She patted her shoulder again.

Then, suddenly, her face tightened. Her eyes bulged out and her teeth clenched. She clawed at her neck, desperately, but her fingernails were unable to gain any purchase against her skin.

After a minute of struggle, her hands flew towards the floor, as though they had just been released. She turned around and ran as fast as she could, plowing through the kitchen doors, leaving them swinging.

"Damn," said Uncle Paul. "I was hoping she'd scream." He whistled, waited a moment, and closed the briefcase.

"Easy trick," Paul said. "Nothing like…"

A squat, middle aged fat man wearing a baseball cap stepped through the door and looked around. He walked up to the counter.

Uncle Paul closed his mouth. His eyes narrowed.

"I don't think anybody's manning the register right now, friend."

The man looked Uncle Paul over with some suspicion, straightened up, and shrugged. "Sign says the place is open. She ain't here right now, I guess I'll have to wait."

He turned towards the cash register and settled into place.

"I'm pretty sure you're wasting your time," Uncle Paul said, but the fat man stayed put.

Paul fingered the clasp on the briefcase.

"Uncle Paul," Andrew interrupted. "Maybe we should leave now and eat while we walk."

He relaxed as his attention moved from the fat man down

to Andrew. A smile crept onto his face.

"You got a point."

6

"You got the right idea." They were walking away from the restaurant, pizza in their hands. It was dusk. "You don't know everything that's going on, but you see things the right way. I can talk to you." He tapped Andrew hard on the forearm. "So here's the deal."

They approached a river and Andrew could see the line where the stores stopped and the houses started up again.

"We have a lot to review, the two of us, later on. But that's later on. Right now, I need you to stay away from that park. Stay away from him. Can you do that for me, Andrew?"

It came to him in between bites, as they reached the apex of the bridge. It had swelled like a balloon in his brain, ready to pop. He had to say it.

"Her."

Paul stopped. "Excuse me?"

"Shadow's a her."

"You gave it a name?"

For a moment he was more embarrassed than afraid. Paul slapped him in the face and he fell hard, driven down towards the pavement like a hammer in a man's hand.

"You gave it a name, you fucking kid… shit…"

Paul ran off.

Andrew watched him go, listened to his footsteps after he turned the corner. The birds on the river shore were singing and the water was cascading over the top of a small dam a few hundred yards away.

He got up once he was sure that Paul was gone. It took him a moment to figure out what to do. He remembered the direction that Paul had taken him from the park, tried to reverse the route in his mind. He started jogging.

When he finally made it to the gazebo, there was a hold on the side of it were a few boards had been pried off. He looked inside.

"Shadow!"

The hole was empty.

He ran home to his grandmother's house.

7

The next morning, Andrew got out of bed, got dressed, ate breakfast, and walked to school. The house was empty as he moved through it.

When he arrived, the students were standing in the playground. His teacher rushed out and grabbed him by the forearm. She brought him through an opening in the chain-link fence that surrounded the school and placed him in line with the rest of his class.

They were taken into the building, one row at a time, down a flight of stairs and into the basement. The lights were dim, the bulbs covered with dust. All Andrew could see were shelves, old desks, electrical boxes, warning signs.

By the time Andrew reached the bottom, the rest of the basement had already been filled. There was a long line of students in front of him and a teacher behind him, blocking the exit. The students were issued instructions. Andrew got down on his knees and covered his head with his hands.

The teacher by the stairs was listening to the radio. She'd set the volume very low, so that the students wouldn't be able to hear it, but Andrew still could. Static burst through the transmission.

"Stay in your homes…"

"…emergency services…"

"…several feet off the ground…"

"…yellow, also green…"

"…we're being… it's…"

"… ambulances, firefighters, and police…"

"… decayed… raining…"

"I don't know what to tell you people at home…"

"… come alive…"

"… my God…"

Time passed. The radio began to yield less disturbance, but although the words were clearer, the people on the other end had less to say. Whatever had happened was finished now.

Andrew looked up at his teacher. Her hands had been clenched around her kneecaps and had now loosened, unconsciously, like a piece of rubber shrinking or expanding to answer the temperature.

She looked down at him.

"Stand up, Andrew," she said. "Time to go."

8

The students were led back upstairs. There was a fleet of cars surrounding the school, their parents waiting for them. Andrew was able to slip away without anyone noticing. He ran home through familiar streets.

His grandmother was sitting in the front living room, watching television. She turned her head as Andrew came through the front door and stared at him like he were something supernatural, an angel from heaven. He walked over to her side and put his hand on her shoulder. She squeezed it as hard as she could.

They were showing pictures of downtown, the same downtown his Uncle Paul had brought him to last night. He hardly recognized it. The buildings had been cut into geometric pieces and reassembled, incorrectly but with a strange precision, as though a plan had been set in motion and then abandoned. The street was lined with tall glass cylinders. The sidewalk oozed back and forth like melted wax down the side of a candle. Everywhere there was smoke.

The men and women living and working within the radius of the destruction were unharmed – they had found themselves suddenly elsewhere, with no memory of how they'd been transported or what had taken place. There'd been only one person to rescue, a man they'd found standing in the middle of a major intersection. He was physically unharmed, but otherwise obliterated. He was mute, unresponding. They had to carry him away on a stretcher. They showed a picture of the man's face. It was Uncle Paul. The ice in his eyes had melted.

9

Andrew waited until his grandmother went to bed and snuck out, went to the park. The hole in the wall was gone. He walked up to the gazebo and brushed his fingertips against the paint. The gateway appeared, and he slipped through it.

The lighting within the chamber had not changed – it seemed more solid, more permanent, than the walls themselves. Shadow was there, in her usual place. Andrew approached her. He could hear her thinking. Her voice appeared in his left ear.

"How are you, Andrew?"

"Shadow, what happened?"

She was quiet for a long time. The dull moan coming from her fingers grew softer. Only when it had become inaudible did she begin to speak.

"Your Uncle Paul came back. He tried to give me instructions, but he already knew that he wasn't going to be able to just tell me what to do."

"He tried to convince me to help him. He said that there were things he could teach me, things only he could know. He brought me outside to show me. It was interesting, but he started showing me ways to hurt people and I didn't want to do that. I was scared."

"I was scared that you wouldn't want to be my friend anymore."

"He got mad at me, and we fought. I tried not to hurt him too much, only as much as I had to…"

Shadow's neck had nearly doubled over, burying her head beneath the surface of her body.

Andrew exhaled. "I'm still your friend, Shadow. He would've hurt other people if you hadn't hurt him. What you did was okay."

Shadow's neck began to straighten itself out.

"Do you want to play chess?" Andrew asked.

They played until it was time for Andrew to go home. Shadow won every game.

The Walk Home

Dominique made lists. It was just how he thought. Starting at his new school that September, he listed the differences. His old school was a charter school. It had fewer than a hundred students and it didn't even look like a school from the outside, if you missed the little sign out front with the books and the little cartoon report card you'd think it was an office. His new school was giant, three stories high, two-thousand students, old, crumbling stone, ledges, gargoyles, people's names on the walls that you couldn't read anymore because the letters had been worn away. There were stories, legends, the ghost in the library, the tunnel in the basement that led to the library across the street.

And there was a football team, which was the reason he was here. His father was not prone to sharing his feelings, but his expectations were never less than clear, and shortly after the death of Dominique's older brother his expectations changed dramatically. The technology academy experiment had come to an end. Dominique was going to become a member of the football team and that was going to be his focus moving forward.

"I changed shifts," his father had said. "I'm picking you up from that school at 6:15, right after practice gets out. In two weeks if you're not on that team you're walking home."

Dominique tried out for the team. He liked his chances at first. Dominique could sprint. He could throw. He could catch.

He could get hit and get back up again. But it all fell apart during scrimmage. There was just too much going on. He kept trying to slow it down in his head, to organize events as they were unfolding, and by the time he did the situation was different and he was doing something that looked stupid. He held out hope that he might at least make the second string, but when the printout appeared on the team bulletin board his name was nowhere on it.

There was no yelling, no punishments. He just ceased to exist. His father's attention shifted to his younger brother. Dominique was left in limbo. He could count on a warm place to sleep and three meals a day, but that was it. He hadn't made the team.

And he had to walk home. He'd hoped that his new school would have a better selection of after-school activities than his old one, but other than athletics and a theater club (any involvement with which would destroy any hope of ever again enjoying his father's respect), his only remaining option was to sit in the public library next door for three hours, which he knew he wasn't going to be able to do. There were no convenient el stops and he'd have to transfer three times to take the bus. He didn't even have a safe place to keep his skateboard at school, his locker was too small and there wasn't anywhere else.

The shortest route back to Dominique's house passed three food and liquor stores, a place where you could buy a soda or a burger or anything that was fried, two churches, the wreckage of a third church that was being rebuilt, a set of unused train tracks buried under layers of weeds, and a music and guitar shop with thick iron cages over the windows and a security camera watching the main entrance. If he went straight home and kept up a quick pace, he could make the walk in forty-five minutes.

He walked home on Monday, Tuesday, Wednesday. Nothing happened, nothing happened, nothing happened. On Thursday, something happened. When he saw them he was about a mile away from the school, walking along the very narrow sidewalk alongside a tall curving gray concrete wall. Tunnels poked through periodically, some of them well-travelled and supported by bridges and walkways, others that were completely boarded up and smelled like urine, and some that were somewhere in between that led to parking lots or vacant lots or piles of gravel.

Three guys, all older than he was, probably seniors if they were still in school. Two of them were bigger than he was but somehow the skinny one was the leader, the one who held the bottle. Dominique saw them in one of the dead-end alcoves as he passed it, sitting on a chunk of concrete and talking to each other quietly like they were sharing a secret.

He took a long glance at them as he walked by. Maybe he looked too long and that was what set it off. Maybe not. No way to tell. He heard them move out of the alcove as he passed, but he didn't look over his shoulder. Not because they might not be there, but because they might be watching and think he was a pussy. He knew it was ridiculous. His father's face at dinner covered everything like wallpaper, facing in from every direction.

He never did figure out how they got in front of him. He walked past another of the alcoves and one of the big guys reached out from around the corner and grabbed him, pulled him in to where the other two were waiting. The tunnel was blocked by a pile of shattered bricks taller than any of them; it was like they had a room to themselves. One of the big guys punched him hard in the stomach and Dominique doubled over, smelled the acid juice of his guts rising up into his throat. The little guy said something; Dominique didn't hear what it was, the other big guy pushed him over and kicked him. They both kicked him. The skinny one didn't join in until there was nothing Dominique could do to defend himself, and even then he jumped in and out, sneaking in a hit and pulling out to call him names.

"Bitch." That was the one Dominique heard and comprehended over the pain and the adrenaline. Not even anything original. That was what stayed with him, what played in his head later.

It felt like longer than it actually took. They pulled his wallet out of his pants and left. He laid on the ground for a little while longer, got up, wiped some dirt off his face, and finished his walk home. His father wasn't home yet. He wasn't even late.

He looked at himself in the mirror, finished washing off. It was mostly his ribs that were sore, his face was fine. His cheek was maybe a little swollen, and you'd have to look close to even notice that. Which he knew his father wouldn't.

"Bitch."

Dominique did the math, knew that the person saying it didn't even have the courage to join in on a three-on-one beating until the other two got it started. It didn't matter. All he heard was what the asshole had said.

Dominique thought about his brother. There was still the remnants of a shrine on the street corner where the car had hit him, wilting flowers and a picture nailed to a fence. Dominique's father never talked about what had happened and Dominique's mother and younger brother took the hint. It took Dominique longer. He had no way to get out to the cemetery where Michael had been buried, but for a few weeks he visited that corner every Sunday afternoon. At some point, he'd stopped.

The possibility occurred to him that that was why he'd gotten jumped, that it was payback for not thinking about his brother often enough. He knew that was bullshit. There were three of them and one of him and they felt like beating on somebody. There was no further truth to it than that.

It would've helped if he'd had someone to say it out loud to. He did the best he could. He ate dinner with his family, slept, got up in the morning, went to school, did his day.

As he walked home, it happened again.

This time, he never saw them coming. He was walking along the wall, further up than before, trying to find a different way through so that he wouldn't have to go through the same area as last time, but it didn't work, they found him anyway. He had a lot of homework that day, his backpack was heavy. One good pull and he went spilling backwards.

If the skinny one called him names, he didn't hear them. They didn't steal anything. They just kicked him in the ribs a few times, laughed at him, and left.

Once they were gone, he didn't move. He just laid there on the sidewalk, imagining that he was still in bed and that this wasn't happening. It took an old Chinese lady on a bicycle coming towards him to inspire him to get up and out of the way.

When he got home, he took off his backpack and looked in his bedroom mirror. There was a long scrape along his right cheek. It was impossible to mistake or ignore. There wasn't anything he could do to cover it up.

He was going to sit down to dinner, looking just like this. It was what was going to happen, like the weather. He wasn't even making a choice.

An hour later, Dominique's family sat down at the dinner table in the same formation they had before his brother had died. They didn't have his chair at the table anymore, but Dominique's mother and younger brother never moved any closer to each other around the table to complete the circuit.

Dominique sat next to his father. Meatloaf tonight, crunchy edges and barbecue sauce. They ate silently. Dominique's father didn't like small talk. If there was to be any conversation it would begin with him.

Twenty minutes after they began, Dominique's father looked up from his plate, at Dominique's face. He looked surprised, as though Dominique had only suddenly appeared.

"Again?"

He chuckled to himself, shook his head the way you would if you saw on the news that something crazy and silly had happened. He didn't say anything after that for a while, and when he did speak up he was asking Dominique's younger brother about how the game had gone.

Dominique couldn't see, couldn't find himself. He closed his eyes and opened them and he was lying under a thin sheet in his room, the digital clock on his dresser shining midnight at him. He should be asleep. He didn't know what had happened to the time, if things were going to start happening in order again. The way things were supposed to happen.

The world was red, like a horror movie.

And finally his brain came to life, slowly but desperately, and he remembered finishing his meal and leaving the table early and going to his room and sitting and staring at the wall for a long time before he went to bed and didn't sleep.

He'd die, if something didn't change. He'd be extinguished.

He woke up in the morning refreshed, as though he'd dreamed. He took a steak knife from a drawer of the kitchen and put it in the sleeve of his coat, before he got in his Mom's car to go to school.

At the end of the day, he walked back home, tracing the long gray wall. He was halfway to the crossing tunnel when they came out from around the corner and lazily surrounded him. The two big ones were behind either shoulder. The skinny one was in front, still close enough to act like he was really getting in Dominique's face, but not so close he couldn't take a step back if anything happened.

He said something to Dominique that Dominique only received as a low roar. Dominique took the knife out of his sleeve. The skinny one stopped talking mid-sentence. There was a pregnant moment, and then action.

The world became strange, like it had the night before, only more so. Incidents flowed together. It was nighttime all the time now, and Dominique was always running. Not running away. Chasing. Hunting. He moved effortlessly, as though the world was on a tilt and he was falling forward, left and right, rushing around corners.

He was still holding the knife. The later at night it was, the more likely it was that they'd notice as he approached, and run. The knife was hot in his hand, and comfortable.

He went back to his school, his old one and the new one both, only to find the halls empty. Once, he found some students from the theater crew who'd hid and stayed overnight to finish building a set. He showed himself to them and chased them around the building for a few minutes, then left. They talked about him; everyone knew it was just another silly ghost story, but they kept telling it anyway.

He could hear them in his left ear, his name in whispers, even as he ran through the night, far from them. He liked how it sounded, his name on their tongues.

One night, he was running along the edge of the wall where he'd been mugged, and came across a picture of himself on the sidewalk, surrounded by faded flowers. On a piece of paper under the photograph was his name, the year he was born, and the year he'd died.

The world shifted again, temporarily, like a cloud crossing the sun making the sky go dark, and he could remember.

He pulled out the knife, the leader jumping back and then running. The big one on the left grabbing him, him turning, cutting. Both of them yelling, terrified, hitting and hitting and hitting, like the water was rising and they didn't know how to swim, and the one heavy rubber boot sole coming down hard on the side of Dominique's head. Stepping away from his body, running.

He didn't know how long this reprieve would last, only that he would forget again, and that he wouldn't come back this time.

He wondered if his older brother had had a moment like this, if he'd come across his own shrine and had time to reflect. And then Dominique thought about his younger brother, what was going to happen now that Dominique was gone.

Dominique looked down at the cutting edge, the point facing forward. He didn't know what would happen if he caught someone. He'd only ever let them run away.

He looked up again and felt himself disappearing, the edges of his silhouette vanishing in the bright light of his decision.

He took a step in the direction of his father's house.

Story Notes

In The Fall

This might be my favorite story that I've written, which makes me feel bad there isn't a more straightforward story of where the idea came from, but it's actually a good example of how ideas actually get assembled, which is to say randomly and in no particular order. Reading Andrew Vachss, talking to Patty Templeton on my podcast about the importance of female characters that can be hated, thinking a lot about how so many horror stories boil down to "what's the monster", working a political job in Wisconsin that had me alternately weaving through trailer parks and making long walks up to peoples' mansions. I don't know if the "different seasons" idea was something I lifted from mythology or just something I thought would seem like it had been, but I carried that idea around for a long time too. I needed something autumn-themed for an actor to perform and wrote this on a tight deadline. Within an hour of finishing, I got an e-mail telling me that the performance was cancelled.

The Sasquatch Vs. Chupacabra Variations 1-9

I'd been threatening to write "Sasquatch Vs. Chupacabra" for a while, and when I finally got down to doing it, I realized I couldn't think of any single idea that did justice to the concept.

Spirits of the Wind

Three things that came together: I got my car towed and got into a conversation with the driver, and couldn't help but wonder how he'd get along with one of my female friends. I'd been wanting to do something playing on "A Midsummer Night's Dream" (although I don't think that's what I actually ended up with). And I wanted to write the jazz club scenes. I tend to use music as a way to find my way into characters, which means I end up writing about "music I've used as a tool and learned to appreciate" as opposed to my own favorites. Fred Anderson, who owned the Velvet Lounge, and Von Freeman had both passed away by the time I got around to writing this, to the extent that people like that ever really do. Both the Velvet and the New Apartment Lounge no longer feature music, but I get my fix at Constellation these days.

A Day And Two Nights When I Was Twenty

As is probably become clear, there's usually a gap of a few years between me experiencing something and me using it in a story. The window eventually passes, which means this might be the last thing I set in a thinly veiled version of Beloit College, at least for a while. I don't know how much the "plastic ghost knocking someone to their death" detail stands out as something too weird to not be true, but it did happen to me and some friends of mine, and if the trajectory of the ghost had been a little different one or the other of us could have been killed.

The Return of Uncle Hungry's Pizza Time Fun Band

Written for the Tamale Hut Cafe First Annual Short Story Contest. I'm glad this made its way out into the world before they release the film adaptation of "Five Nights At Freddie's", a franchise I only became aware of after this story was completed. The band in this story used to play at "Enchanted Castle" in lovely Lombard, IL, and still decorated their dining room for a few years after they stopped using it.

I-65

Only two big pieces this time, one of which was visiting my friend and fellow author Hunter C. Eden when he lived in Nashville. I also worked the building and grounds department at my old high school during my college summers. It was a good job that still made me happy not to be doing manual labor as a career, if for no other reason than I'm sure the school has started subcontracting out the work since then. One of the lifers retired during the summer when I worked there and came back a few weeks later to show off his car. The bartender in this story is either Gary from my Charlie Harmer stories or a close relative.

Two Nights Only

The theater is pretty clearly the DuPage Theater, formerly in downtown Lombard, which stood in Historical Society limbo throughout my childhood. I never saw the interior, even though it was common knowledge among my peers growing up that it wasn't tricky to get in there. Good honors student that I was, I always tried to keep my recreational trespassing short of breaking and entering.

PCBF

My friend Ben was the organizer of a Transhumanist student organization, and in supporting him I came into contact with people who, in my humble Philosophy-major opinion, were being really optimistic about their ability to figure out what a full-fledged artificial intelligence would want or how one would behave. I've never been to Florida.

Wetwork

This story is a little older than most of the others in this volume, and I think of it as a cousin to "Quiet" from my last collection. I'd been feeling uncomfortable with the whole "person who makes the hard choices" thing that had seemed to be coming up a lot in my little corner of popular culture, and I was curious how far that could be taken before people would lose sympathy with the hard-decider, so I tried this out. A friend of mine who worked on boats a lot told me about a guy she'd worked with who'd aged out of his ability to be anything except the cook, and who went exclusively by an obscene nickname. I'm pretty sure that "Fuckmeat" was something I made up, and I don't remember what the guy's real title actually was, but I don't think I exaggerated the profanity by all that much.

The Envelope Job

Let me know if you like this one. I have plans for our friend Byron, maybe some pretty ambitious plans, and I'm curious what people think of him.

Ebb Tide

The other Beloit College story in this collection. The original concept was really different and involved historically accurate pirate battles. It strayed enough that I could probably try the initial idea again if I wanted without appearing to repeat myself.

The Gardener Estate

This is a fun story to perform, limited only by the fact that I am not Gilbert Gottfried. It's fun when you get a mixed response to a story because the basic concept disagrees with how some people think the world works. I've had people tell me point blank that it doesn't make sense that Theo would spend his time the way he does if he wasn't enjoying himself. I think the Hugh Hefner reference covers that, personally, but it's interesting to see what other people think. The character "Debbi" was named after a supporter of the Kickstarter for my last collection, whom she otherwise does not resemble.

Blue Eyes

I'd had Jekyll and Hyde on my little mental list of things I'd wanted to play with sooner or later. I'd originally thought about doing something on a larger scale and having a whole town in the middle of nowhere off the highway where every house had a room in their basement, but I needed something short for a performance and it turns out that the whole thing works much better as something more intimate.

The Specimen

I could have mentioned ninjas in this story. It breaks my heart that Ninjitsu is bullshit.

Shadow

All right, I sort of lied. This isn't a Beloit College story, but it's definitely a Beloit story. This was the first story I wrote when I first decided to get serious about cranking out short fiction and trying to sell it. It was also the first chapter of a novel for a long time prior to some revisions that split it up between the second and third chapters instead.

The Walk Home

Like I said before, I tend to find myself writing about things from my own life about five years after they happen on a pretty consistent schedule. If things keep going that way, I've got at least a few more south side stories ahead of me. What freaks me out about the source material for this story was not that I had to have the "taking a knife to school is a bad idea" conversation, but that I found myself doing things like that frequently enough that it didn't even seem like that big a deal at the time. My father likes this story a lot.

A little less than a year ago as I write this, I quit my job to write full time. It's gone better than I had any right to hope and a big part of that is the amazing people I'm lucky enough to have around me. All the thanks in the world to my family and friends.

Many thanks to Xavier Nuez for the use of the awesome photograph on the cover. You can see more of his work over at www.nuez.com.

Just about all of these stories were first heard at different reading series in the lovely city of Chicago. I'm a frequent flier at Gumbo Fiction Salon, Tamale Hut Cafe Presents, and Pungent Parlor, and if you like the stories in this book there's a good chance you'd like those events. I also run the mighty Bad Grammar Theater, which has been going strong for a few years now and meets every third Friday of the month in the mysterious back room of Powells Books at the corner of Roosevelt and Halsted. Come on by and say hello anytime.

www.badgrammartheater.com

www.brendandetzner.com